For Michael!
One of my favorite people at Selectron!
Happy Reading

Dielle & Jeff

Sambuka Black

By
Dielle Alexandre and Jeff Mulcaster

Published by Chez Champignon

Copyright © 2011

ISBN 978-0-9836115-0-9

www.chezchampignon.com

www.sambukablack.com

5% of proceeds go to
ferret rescue and adoption

Made in Oregon, USA
Printed by Oregon Litho, McMinnville, OR

GimPhoto.net was used to edit the illustrations. It is a freeware program well worth paying for.

Back Cover Portrait of the Authors:
character design by JR Williams
airbrushed by Damian Zari

This book is dedicated to my mom who taught me the most important thing in life is to be happy and the best way to achieve that is to be a good person, and to my beloved Jeffrey "Duncan" Mulcaster who makes me happy, helps me be a good person and without whom, Sambuka Black would never have been born. Dielle.

dedicated to my dear friend, zeta gaudet, for decades of understanding and encouragement, and to my precious little faun, dielle, for her unending patience, creativity and optimism. she's the real reason this project happened. jeff.

Table of Contents

Prologue 1

A Dragon's Tale 14

A Gift from Gran 25

Bug Patrol 37

A Show at the Carnivale 45

The Plan 56

Mythical Creatures 66

The Real Story 76

Sexapus 90

Dinner 100

Logues' Bridge 110

Logue's Butte 121

The Depths 133

Fishing and Camping 142

Stopping Here 155

Northern Port City 163

The Auction 174

The Minister's Lair 183

Aftermath 202

Epilogue 209

Map of Kanadan

Aquifer Diagram

Mom's Shelf

Math Puzzle Explanation

Chez Champignon Books

Kyle's Original Poem

Things to Ponder

Sambuka Black

Flames exploded.

Out of the inferno rolled a straw haired, scruffy jawed man with a jewel encrusted eye patch. Behind him was an enormous green dragon, chained to a rocky cave wall and spewing fire. Two leather clad guards positioned on overhead scaffolding shot crossbows at a petite purple satyr as she leapt over a gap in the wooden planks. A brutish four-armed cyclops strained against the dragon's leash and the man, engulfed in flames and running blindly, ran out of dock and plunged into the chilly water below.

Sambuka Black

The immense iron anchor plunged into the chilly water below and sank to the rocky seabed. Slightly disturbed crabs scuttled aside, fish darted between timber pilings, and three pair of legs, human, satyr, and cyclops, slowly kicked as they protruded from the underside of a large hollow log. From above, the log appeared to slowly drift past several sailing vessels and around a heavy barge before making its way into the mountain's cavernous aquatic loading dock.

The dragon calmly blew puffs of flame onto a soot-blackened boiler. His right wing badly deformed, his eyes gray and lifeless, the creature's movements were dazed and slow.

Prologue

Nearby, a creaking conveyor belt transported sides of butchered meat on hooks as workers hauled heavy crates out to the loading area. Two finely dressed men, ghostly in the torchlight, strolled past the stacks of outgoing goods.

The dark haired, bearded and rotund Minister Bell was laughing and gesturing wildly, his extravagant robes swirling, his fingers filled with gold rings and fluttering about.

"...on her shoes! Wheel of Doom indeed!"

"But overall an enjoyable experience?" asked his tall, blond colleague, Secretary James, his hands efficiently clasped behind his back.

"Oh yes. All was forgotten the moment the next young man walked by. Takes after her mother! Who made me swear to thank you profusely for that beautiful mirror, by the way. Such craftsmanship!"

"From expert artisans in the far east," replied the Secretary, the faintest hint of pride in his thin smile, "our best trading partners. Speaking of, the loading is almost complete. A full shipment, very profitable. Barring bad weather, they set sail tomorrow."

The two men stepped into daylight and followed the walkway outside to a three masted cargo ship anchored in the bay.

"Excellent work once again, mon ami. These last many years have been very good to us, and the people of this land. We all owe you a great debt."

"You are too kind, Minister," deferred the Secretary.

They watched as workers finished loading the ship. Several small red dragons were herded up the gangplank and a cage full of huge buzzing wasps swung by on a towering, dragon-powered crane. Admiring the inventory, Minister Bell remarked, "Ahh, such succulent specimens. What a delicacy! I don't know how I ever enjoyed life without them. It's amazing you can still find them ranging free."

"It is a vast country," replied the Secretary, "much wilderness yet to be explored."

"True, very true," he agreed, still licking his lips. "Of course, thanks to your domestic breeding programs, we never go wanting." The Minister patted his presumably satisfied stomach and gave the Secretary a hedonistic wink.

"The butchery licensing has proved very successful," said Secretary James, "All but the smallest villages have thriving industry."

"Well done, well done. When the citizenry is happy, we're happy, eh?"

"Yes sir," replied his loyal second-in-command as they reached the end of the dock.

"As always, a pleasure Mr. Secretary. I really must visit more often. This northern air is most bracing and a boon to my constitution, not to

Prologue

mention my appetite." Minister Bell's smile was contagious, but landed uncomfortably on the Secretary's face.

"You are always most welcome." Turning to one of the guards, he ordered, "You there, please assist the Minister with his flyer and belongings."

"Yes sir!" barked the guard, jumping to task.

The Secretary turned back with a gracious bow, "Au Revoir, I wish you an uneventful trip home."

The Minister arranged himself awkwardly on his immense blue dragon, saluted dramatically, and barely managed to announce his destination before the dull eyed creature launched itself into the air.

After the guards passed by, three damp sneaky heads peeked out from behind the carefully stacked wooden crates.

The man gestured with a nod, whispering, "Let's go, now's our chance!" before bolting for the back of the cave.

The one-eyed, one-horned and hugely muscled cyclops hesitated, "No, wait! I can still see them."

"C'mon ya big baby," piped the faun girl, "just keep your giant noggin down. It'll be a lot worse than the jailor's lash if we're caught again." She trotted away but waved back at him, pointing urgently toward the end of the dragon's chain where it attached to the rock wall. He sighed, nervously snuck over, and began filing through the metal restraint.

An underlying stench of sulfur caused the man's nostrils to flare as he reverently moved forward, careful not to tread on a heavily clawed and lethal looking foot. He reached up and gently placed his palms on the dragon's shoulder then, hearing hoofsteps, looked back and said quietly, "Alex, go over to the entrance and watch for guards." She nodded and scampered away. He closed his good eye, bowed his head and mumbled rhythmically.

As Alex approached the mouth of the cave, Secretary James stepped in. Green like a cat's but dead at the same time, his eyes narrowed and one word seethed from between his clenched teeth, "Thieves." He clutched a fistful of air then flung it savagely aside.

The man lifted from the ground and was hurled against the moving conveyor belt, an iron hook bursting out the front of his vest. He stared down in disbelief, waiting for the rush of pain, dangling and kicking as he was taken back toward the slaughterhouse in the belly of the mountain.

"Silas!" screamed Alex, rooted to the spot and looking around in a panic.

The Secretary waved his hand and the dragon

Prologue

Sambuka Black

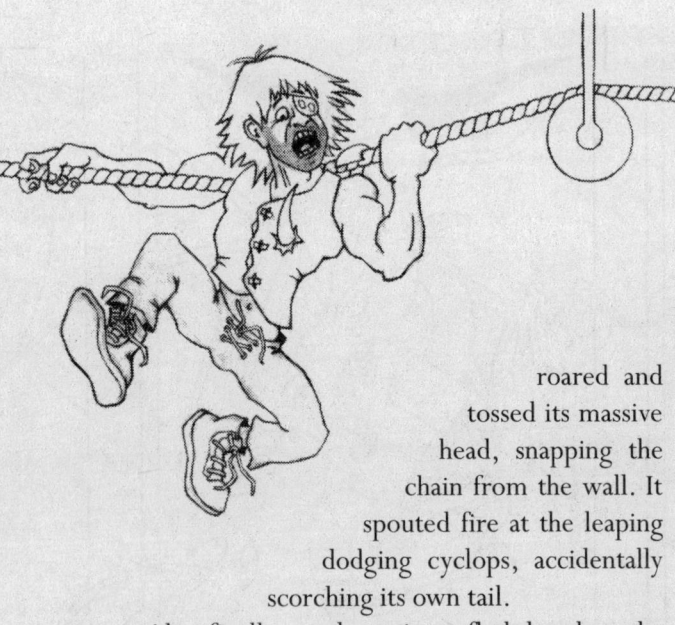

roared and tossed its massive head, snapping the chain from the wall. It spouted fire at the leaping dodging cyclops, accidentally scorching its own tail.

Alex finally acted, tossing a flash bomb at the Secretary's feet. While he was temporarily blinded, she grabbed a melon sized crystal ball from a nearby alcove and hurled it as well. Squinting through the smoke and reacting too late, his long slender arms closed on nothing and he watched helplessly as his precious crystal shattered against the floor.

Alex dashed away, backhandedly flinging her spinning bolas. Finding their mark, the counter swinging weights nicely wrapped the Secretary's wrists in twine.

"Guards!" he shouted, entangled and furious.

Prologue

Silas, too, was still entangled and continued to struggle on the hook. Gripping the belt above his head, he swung his legs up and hung by his knees, then, with his right hand, eased the curving piece of metal out from under his left arm.

He dropped to the ground and sprinted behind the boiler, growling, "This is gonna be more difficult than I thought."

The cyclops had caught the dragon's leash, his fingers woven through the cold iron links, and was being violently swung about, his left arms pin wheeling wildly.

"Duncan!" cried Alex, bounding back toward her cohorts as two armed and armored guards ran along the overhead scaffolding.

Avoiding the dangerously swinging chain and gouts of flame, the chaos dancing fiercely across the rubies of his eye patch, Silas again pressed his hands against the scaly skin and chanted his mantra.

The dragon's opaque eyes began to clear to a brilliant sparkling yellow and his deep voice rumbled throughout the cavern,

Where am I? I remember fire. Falling. Pain. Aaarh! Why does my tail hurt!?

"Careful of the beast!" shrieked the Minister as crossbow bolts impaled crates and posts and beams indiscriminately.

"It's working!" Alex called, just as a speeding bolt pierced Silas' shoulder. Looking down in shock yet again, he scowled at the bloody protruding point. As the floor rushed up to meet his knees, the dragon's eyes clouded over and torrents of fire once more flooded the chamber.

He struggled back to his feet and dove to protect Alex but part of her back was instantly charred and most of her hair melted to a matted sticky mess. With the force of a falling tree, the sweeping green tail slammed into her kneeling body and she sprawled, bleeding and broken. Silas, engulfed in flames and running blindly, plunged off the dock.

Grunting and straining, Duncan yanked the chain around a thick wooden post, slamming the dragon's head against it, then wrapped it again and again immobilizing the fire spitting mouth.

In a slow daze, Alex raised her hand, carefully studying the eye patch that dangled from her fingers. The smooth granite floor was slippery under her sharp hooves and she warmly accepted Duncan's familiar arms around her waist. Floating weightless beside him, she didn't notice his gait was staggered by the feathered bolt sunk deep in his thigh.

Confronted by the silhouettes of three more guards, Duncan desperately scanned the water for a sign of Silas and, hopeful, saw their log slowly

Prologue

drifting away. He turned and fled deeper into the depths of the cave.

Finally free of his bonds, the Secretary, with one hand, fished the whimpering Silas from the water like so much wet laundry and easily drug him along as he inspected the dragon for damage.

"Did you really think I would let you steal such a valuable commodity?" he inquired coldly.

"Not stealing...needs to be free," was all that choked out of Silas' blistered throat.

"Yes, yes, of course. I'm certain your motives were purely altruistic."

"You don't understa-"

"You don't understand that you will soon suffer for your indiscretion!"

The guards barked out commands as they pursued the hobbled cyclops. Even wounded, Duncan outpaced them, his powerful legs propelling him onward through a labyrinth of tunnels, up stone stairways, past barred doors, and out an opening high above the cavern. The startled doorman jumped back as Alex tore open a small paper package releasing dozens of pink butterflies. He threw up his hands and heard a sound like a sail unfurling and when the cloud of insects dispersed, the strangers were gone.

A sailor, hearing adamant footsteps and guttural moans, looked up from his packing.

"This miscreant will make a fine addition to the feed supply. Throw him in with the wasps," the Secretary calmly instructed.

"In with the wasps?" he gaped.

"Are you questioning my order?"

"No sir. Right away sir."

Duncan and Alex, on top of a nearby building, watched, paralyzed, as Silas was forced into the cage with the giant wasps. They immediately swarmed, stinging and biting.

Alex lunged forward but Duncan restrained her, putting a hand over her mouth, "Stop! You have to be quiet! We can't help him now."

Silas thrashed and screamed for several long seconds, then all was quiet.

Duncan gently released the distraught Alex who stared, devastated, tears streaming down her face.

"It's all my fault. Everything."

"We have to go. They'll be coming for us," he urged, pulling her along, the day's last rays of sun fading as they climbed from the roof.

Prologue

A Dragon's Tale

There once was a mighty dragon
Who lived on a mountaintop
He would wail and wail and wail all night
And simply would not stop

One day came a knight
All shiny and bright
Upon his silver steed
All dressed in white
His sword held tight
To do the Noble Deed

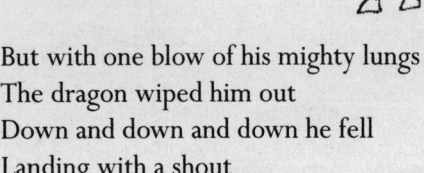

But with one blow of his mighty lungs
The dragon wiped him out
Down and down and down he fell
Landing with a shout

"I'll get you dragon, I'll get you yet
You've not seen the last of me!"
Again and again and again he tried
'Til he was blown right out to sea

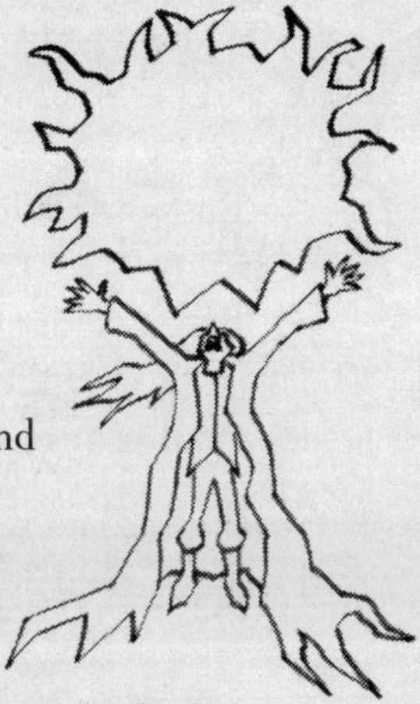

A Dragon's Tale

But then came a wizard
To kill that lizard
His magical wand in hand
The village agreed
That he would succeed
For he was the best in the land

He conjured all night
Till he could ignite
A roaring fireball
Higher and higher and higher it climbed
Till it reached ten feet tall

But the wizard annoyed the dragon
So he raised a mighty din
And he dug and he dug and he dug a huge hole
And dropped the wizard in

But the wizard wasn't beaten
And he cast an awesome spell
"Get thee down thou unclean beast
Your wailing I will quell"
And he hypnotized the scaly thing
And took away its will

Sambuka Black

Four-year-old Kara was tucked in bed, wide eyed and a bit upset as her father closed the storybook.

"But why Dad? Why were they so mean to the dragon?"

"Because dragons are big scary monsters who'd eat us up if the Minister didn't protect us. But he does so that little girls like you can go to sleep and have happy dreams."

Kara blinked back tears, "Well, I think he's mean. If I saw a dragon crying, I'd want to know why."

"Somehow, I don't doubt that," Dad chuckled. "Goodnight Sweetheart."

Nine-year-old Kara sat up in bed, rubbed the sleep out of her bleary eyes and blinked in the mid-morning sun.

Her bedroom was round and made of large granite blocks. Shelves lined the walls and were crowded with puzzles, mechanical wooden toys, odd shaped rocks and other various treasures precious only to her.

Her bookcase had tomes of all sizes, some old and worn, most of them bound in leather, and they covered all sorts of subjects relating to dragons, nature, science and history. One was entitled, *Mythical Creatures - Fantasy and Fairytales*; others included, *Modern Inventions and the Power of Water, Anatomy of Dragons, Mining for Munchkins, A Distant Land in the Desert, History of Magic,* and next to all those was the biggest book of all, *A Dragon's Tale*.

To the other side of the door was a desk cluttered with quills and papers, a sketchbook and charcoal, and on the wall was a map depicting her family's homeland, Kanadan.

Kara had changed out of her night clothes and her short tousled hair had been somewhat brushed when she made her way down the long curving stone staircase and into another round room, her mother's workshop. Shelves filled with tools and small containers lined the walls. There were chisels and augers, hammers and saws, ceramic jars and glass bottles in an array of colors, all neatly labeled with words both common and cryptic. Planes and rasps and files were scattered across the heavy worktable and piles of lumber covered much of the floor.

Mom was kneeling down doing some final sanding on a simple bench. She looked up and smiled as Kara walked in, "Hi Hon!"

Kara plopped down on an older, much fancier bench.

"What time is it?" she asked groggily, squinting at the sun streaming through the window.

"It's almost lunchtime. You slept in extra late this year," Mom said as she got up to close the shutters, a sprinkle of sawdust glinting in her auburn hair. "Now where did I put that buffing cloth?" she pondered, tapping her lip with her finger and looking around.

Yawning and stretching, eyes closed, Kara pointed over to a shelf on the far side of the room.

"For goodness sakes, if my head wasn't glued on. So, are you wishing for a dragon again?"

"Nooo. I'd be happy to just get my magic. Finally."

"Oh Kara, don't worry. You're just a late bloomer like your dad, that's all. It'll happen." Mom turned to the bench, "By the wall." It lifted a couple inches off the ground, floated over to the wall, plopped back down and remained motionless.

"But I'm nine already! Magic is stupid anyways," she humpfed, crossing her arms.

Mom sat down on the family bench and hugged her close. "You have your Gran's power," she offered.

"Great," Kara replied sarcastically, then paused. "Why don't boys get anything passed down?"

"But they do! Men inherit the ability to carry things for us."

Kara snorted, "Don't let Dad hear you say that!"

"And you have your father's math skills," she added, "You like that, puzzles and things?"

"Yeah, but math isn't magic," Kara retorted.

"Don't let your dad hear you say that," Mom smirked.

Kara traced her fingers along the old bench's elaborately carved flowers and vines. "Why don't you carve on your furniture anymore?" she asked.

"Oh, I think your father has enough style for both of us. And besides, people can't really afford fancy things these days anyways. But, I do like carving. Maybe…" she trailed off.

They shared a moment of silent reverie.

"Speaking of your father," Mom started, "how 'bout you run down to the Gaudets' and see if you can drag him back here. Your guests will be arriving soon, after all."

"Yeah! Okay."

As Kara left the house, she looked back over her shoulder and smiled. The stone cottage with the adorably twisted turret looked so cute from the outside and she never got tired of seeing it. Her dad was the best architect in the whole countryside.

Walking along the dirt road, she passed several unhealthy gardens then crossed a small wooden bridge, its clear stream trickling over mossy rocks. The under-construction house with its waterwheel, huge gears, iron chains and several intriguing, yet still unrecognizable features, dwarfed her dad and his two clients.

He was holding design plans while repeatedly lifting and dropping a clipped on strip of paper that showed an addition. Kara couldn't quite make out what they were saying, but could tell from Mme. Gaudet's stiff posture that she was less than excited.

"With, without, with, without." Dad's enthusiasm was bubbling through and he completely missed his client's furrowed brow.

"Really? An exposed spiral elevator?"

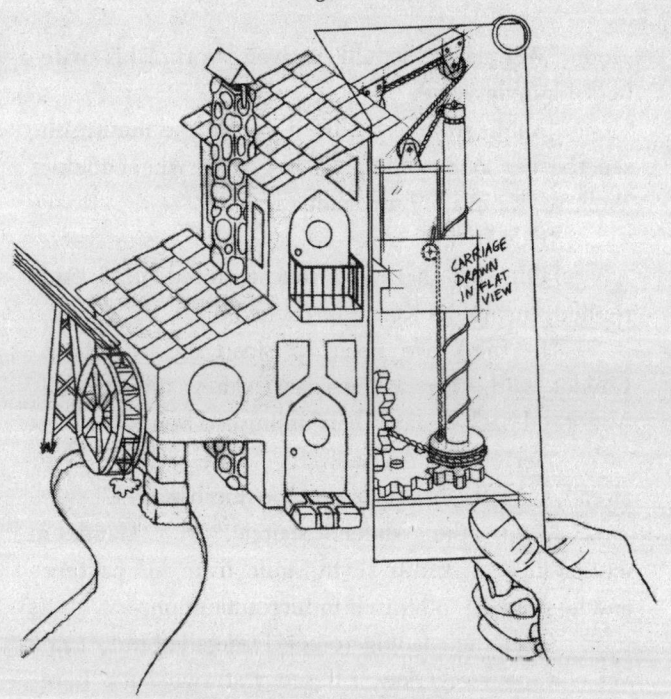

"It would be unique," Dad's eyes were trained on his creation, "and it nicely balances the waterwheel, don't you think?"

"I like it!" exclaimed M. Gaudet, ignoring his mate's dubious expressions.

Emboldened, Dad continued, "I've been wanting to build one of these for a long time now. I'd even throw it in gratis, as a show piece."

"I *really* like it!" said M. Gaudet.

"Well, how would it even work?" his wife begrudgingly asked.

"Ahhh, simple, really! It's all in the math. You see the big axle coming off the waterwheel there? Well, we tie in a big sprocket-"

"Hey Dad."

"Oh, hey there my yellow haired girl," Dad replied, turning as Kara approached.

"I...think we need to sleep on it," Mme. Gaudet said, "for a few days." They turned and wandered back toward their unfinished home.

"Seriously? An elevator?" she asked. "We already have the fire pole, and the dumb waiter."

"And the slider stairs!" M. Gaudet's exuberance coaxed a slight smile from his partner and he grinned to himself in secret triumph.

Over their fading voices, Dad called out, "Oh, yes. Of course. Okay, I'll see you two back here tomorrow then."

Kara's feet scuffed through the gravel as her mind worked. "The crow dropped pebbles in until the water was high enough?"

"Excellent! Okay. Try this one," challenged Dad. "Add 1 plus 2 plus 3 all the way up to 100."

"What?!" barked Kara. "That's impossible! I'd need a-"

"No, no, you can do it in your head. Just think

A Dragon's Tale

a moment…"

"But…okay, wait a second…uuuh…49…plus 100 at the end…5000!"

"Nooo, that's not quite ri-"

"Oh! Plus 50 left over in the middle! 5050!"

"Ha! That's my girl."

As they continued down the road toward home, Kara got quiet for a minute, then asked, "How old were you when you got your power?"

Dad blinked at the unexpected question then said, with an air of nostalgia, "I was eleven. I was so excited! The first enchanted thing I ever built was a doghouse for that magically challenged friend of mine."

"Maybe *I'm* magically challenged," Kara muttered.

haha! dad lost his protractor in his own pocket!

"What? No, obviously not. Come on now," he consoled, putting his arm around her shoulders as they walked along. "Oh wait! Gotta go back. I left my protractor."

"Ya mean this one?" She pulled the fine brass instrument from his back pocket.

"Now how'd that get back there?" he mused bemusedly, shaking his head. "Hey, did your Gran get here yet? I can't wait to see what she's almost wearing this time."

"Dad!" She whacked him playfully on the arm.

"What?! I just meant she's…a very fashionable woman." He paused. "Don't tell her I said that." He paused again. "Or your mother."

A Gift from Gran

Back home, Kara stepped into the kitchen and was immediately showered with kisses and enveloped in the smell of sweet ancient incense. Gran was dressed in an outlandish outfit combining a velvet choker ringed in long exquisite feathers, a tightly laced bustier with a short skirt and a swishy ruffled petticoat, brightly striped stockings, dizzyingly high-heeled boots and, perched on her head, a hat topped with an elaborate, fully functioning, miniature windmill. She was holding an intricately painted and finely engraved vase that displayed an array of magnificent spirally flowers which she promptly presented.

"They're beautiful!" Kara gasped as she took the gift. "Where did you find them?"

"I bought this wonderful little glass greenhouse last season," she gestured something the size of a vegetable basket, "very expensive! But now I can always have flowers with me. I think these would

Sambuka Black.

A Gift from Gran

look especially perfect in your bedroom window." Gran's mischievous smile flew past Mom and Dad, but Kara caught it and grinned back.

Up in her room, she carefully set the fragrant bouquet on her desk then turned around to find Gran offering a cloth bundle tied with string. Taking the package, Kara hopped onto her bed, eagerly unwrapped it and found herself gazing at a book entitled, *The Secret Life of Dragons*.

"Go on, open it," nudged Gran, sitting down beside her, eyes a twinkle.

She turned back the cover revealing blank pages with a circular compartment cut through them. Cradled inside was a clear corked bottle containing a tiny egg. Kara stared, not letting herself believe it. "Is it..." was all she was able to say.

Her grandmother carefully removed the bottle and poured the egg out onto the bedspread where it assumed its actual cantaloupe size.

"Oh Gran," breathed Kara, entranced by the shimmering, swirly purple patterns.

After a moment of shared wonder, Gran broke the silence. "Now, we have to keep this a secret, just between us," she said in an uncharacteristically foreboding tone, "and you have to be very careful. If the egg is out of the bottle for too long, it will hatch, and you know what that would mean, right?"

"Yeah, that would be…bad," Kara replied, equally somber.

"So keep practicing with other things and don't take it out again until you're an expert, okay?"

"I will, I promise! I'll practice every day!"

Gran enchanted the egg back into the bottle and handed it to Kara who lunged for her middle, hugging with all her might.

"Ooh, too tight. I have to pee like a waterfall!" She grimaced theatrically then ran out the door, the little windmill blades spinning.

"I love your hat!" giggled Kara before she again stared wondrously at her best present ever.

She lifted her gaze at the sound of Gran's returning footsteps but was startled to hear her mother's voice. Quickly reaching behind her back, she stuffed the bottle under the edge of her pillow

A Gift from Gran

just as Mom appeared.

"Hey bashful birthday girl, everyone's...oh, what's that?" Kara looked guilty, then glanced at the open book at the foot of her bed.

"Oh, yeah! Uh, it's from Gran! A hidden treasure book. You know, for hiding things!"

"Hmmm. Very mysterious. Well, your guests have arrived and are anxious to see the lady of the day. Would you be willing to grace us with your presence?"

Kara broke into a wide smile, "Okay!"

She bounced off the bed and followed Mom out of the room. There was a small *clink!* then raucous cheers downstairs erupted with the opening chorus of the traditional dirge. Fists pounded out the rhythm and each line was accented by a hefty house shaking stomp.

> Happy birthday (*Stomp!*)
> Happy birthday (*Stomp!*)
> Soon the reaper will arrive
> Chop your head of with his scythe
>
> One year older (*Stomp!*)
> Getting colder (*Stomp!*)
> You are one step closer to
> Rigor mortis claiming you

Happy birthday (*Stomp!*)
Happy birthday (*Stomp!*)
In a coffin, graveyard bound,
They will plant you underground.

One year older (*Stomp!*)
Getting colder (*Stomp!*)
Six feet down and two feet wide,
Worms will dine upon your hide.

Happy birthday *(Stomp!)*
Happy birthday *(Stomp!)*
One short life is all you get,
Better make the best of it.

Happy birthday (*Stomp!*)
Happy birthday (*Stomp!*)

The party went on and on as daylight faded to moonlight and the merry voices slowly wound down to parting wishes and goodbyes.

"Goodnight everyone! Thank you for everything!" Kara's excitement, however, was anything but fading as she ran up to her room and jumped on the bed, humming the Birthday Song. She pulled back the pillow and gasped, then looked over the side of the bed and saw the broken bottle and pieces of purple eggshell.

A Gift from Gran

"Oh, nooo. It fell!"

Surveying the room, she saw bare stems in Gran's vase and a torn open cornhusk doll with its grain innards scattered on the floor.

Faint echoey peeping made her freeze in place. She spied movement under some dirty clothes as footsteps began clunking up the stairs. Quickly throwing more laundry on top of the pile, she spun toward the door just hoping the whole thing stayed still.

Dad knocked, but came in without waiting and slid the well-read storybook from its place on the shelf. "Hey half-pint, ready for our annual Poem reading?"

"Dad!" Kara, distracted with the dragon situation, was rather curt, "Don't you think that story is a bit naïve? People are good; dragons are bad. Is this really the message we want to be sending?" Her hands emphatically on her hips, she was doing her best to get rid of her father when she heard the peeping again.

Dad looked baffled, "Uhhh…"

She tried to drown out the high-pitched chirps. "I mean," her voice rising, "what did the dragon do anyway? He sat on a mountaintop! He wailed too loudly! Maybe he was just lonely? Ever think of that?"

A Gift from Gran

Her eyes darted side to side but the peeping seemed to have stopped.

Dad stared, befuddled, then started to move in reverse, "Okaaay, I'll just back away slowly…" He cautiously set the book down on her desk, "Um, maybe you're too grown up for bedtime stories now."

"I'm sorry. I guess I'm just a little overwhelmed. You know, getting older and everything."

"Yeah, I guess you're more of a five-eighths pint now, huh?" he said with a hopeful smile.

"Daaad," she groaned, rolling her eyes.

"Well, good night then, young lady. Oh! You're not too old for some extra birthday cookies, are you?"

He pulled a full plate out from behind his back and placed it on the desk as well.

"Never! Thanks Dad. Goodnight."

"Happy dreams."

The moment the door closed, Kara dropped to her knees and began gingerly picking through socks and shirts when suddenly, a little purple dragon popped out.

"Oh!" she exclaimed.

He cocked his head, scrambled straight up over Kara's shoulder, clothes flying, and skidded down her back. She whirled around to see him backing up, mouth open, bouncing up and down on all fours as if on hot coals. He was skinny and bony with raptor-like claws, a pointy snout, wrinkly folded wings and a snaking spear tip tail. He looked toothy and vicious, but his movements were puppyish and uncoordinated as he slid into the wall then darted behind the dresser.

Kara sprang to her feet, expecting a dangerous, messy, noisy chase. Instead, the little lizard scampered back out, squatted, wiggled, then leaped into her arms, peeping happily and licking her laughing face.

"Hahahaha! Shhh, little dragon! Shhh. Yes, that's you! Little Dragon!" Her giggles lowered to a whisper, "We have to be quiet!"

Dragon's peeping became softer. He nuzzled her awestruck face, licked her ear, sniffed the air a couple times and then, slowly but purposefully, stretched his neck in the direction of the cookies.

"You're hungry. Of course you're hungry! I guess the flowers were just an appetizer, huh? You want a cookie? Mmmm *cookie*." She sat down on the bed with him and he munched ecstatically.

Cookie! Cookie! Cookie!

Kara jumped, shocked to hear actual words. She tried to shush him again, but then drew back. She plugged her ears and the ambient munching noise was muffled, but Dragon's voice was still clear.

A Gift from Gran

Cookie! Cookie! Cookie!

She plugged her ears again just to make sure.

"Wow," astonishment filled her, "I can hear your thoughts," then, like a punch in the stomach, "Gran's gonna kill me. I am in so much trouble."

She gently pet and scratched him as he finished a couple more cookies.

"But you are so pretty," she crooned.

He stretched his neck as his peeps transitioned into soft trills. Then yawning, his tiny forked tongue curled like a kitten's. He crawled under the covers and Kara followed, snuggling up behind him.

Dawn was breaking through the window as Dad poked his head in the door.

"Morning three-quarter pint!" he announced, adding, "Thought ya mighta grown even more overnight."

Kara jerked awake, frozen in surprise as Dragon stirred under the covers. She hastily recovered, kicking her feet to camouflage his movement, and stammered, "Uhhh...I always have happy feet in the morning."

Dad gave her a weird look, but, "Breakfast is ready," was all that came out. He closed the door, quizzically muttering to himself, "Happy feet?"

Kara got out of bed and pantomimed to Dragon to stay put, whispering, "I'll be back," as she

put the last cookie in front of him and went out. He watched her go, sitting up tall with the sheet draped over his head.

Later, when Kara returned, he was in the same spot but lying down, waiting, his chin resting on his front paws, sheet still on his head, cookie still in front of him.

"Too bad birthdays only come once a year," she said, sitting on the bed and stroking his neck. "It's, 'back to your chores again today.' Bug patrol. Mom and Dad say I'm an expert! Ya know, they have to go work down the road today, you wanna come help me?"

Dragon was excited by all the wonderful attention and began crunching enthusiastically on the cookie.

Bug Patrol

Around back was a shed, a barn and an expansive garden. Plants were growing, but not looking their best. Many had browning leaves and others had small deformed fruits.

Kara bent down and picked up a terra cotta pot and, sneering disgustedly, dumped its slimy contents out onto the ground. She then started digging between the rows of vegetables with a short pointy stick while Dragon followed behind. One at a time, she pulled up squiggling gray grubs and dropped them into the clay pot.

Dragon observed the whole process closely then ran his nose along the ground following an invisible trail. He stopped, wiggled his butt in anticipation, then *Whap!* slammed his nose into the dirt and came up with a grub in his teeth. He looked up at Kara, expectantly.

"Nice!" she exclaimed.

He gobbled it down.

"Eww…" she grimaced.

Sambuka Black

As Dragon continued to hunt and feed, Kara moved on to knocking opalescent beetles off half-eaten leaves and into the pot. They had the same color patterns as the grubs, but with legs and exoskeletons, too. After a while, she started singing a simple song with a folksy tune:

The grubs eat the roots,
So we gotta root 'em out,
Beetles go crunch on the le-e-e-eaves.

First you bite the head off,
Then you suck the guts out,
Then you throw the rest of it awa-a-a-ay.

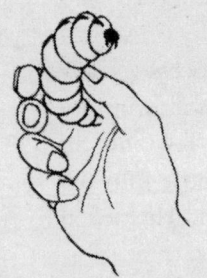

Short squishy squiggly ones,
Creepy crawly crunchy ones,
Yummy nummy tummy filling bugs.

Tummy full, Dragon peeped along, his pitch going up and down with the melody.

Bug Patrol

When she finished her patrol, Kara took the squirming collection of grubs and beetles to the leaky aqueduct behind their house. She held the pot up above her head and caught the drips until it was mostly full. Then she  covered it with a flat piece of bark and shook it a few times, finally setting it on the ground with a rock on top, just for good measure.

Their next chore was at the top of a small rise beyond the garden. As they climbed, Dragon spotted a flitting butterfly and followed its path with his whole head, observing every twist and turn. He wiggled his butt and just when Kara thought he was going to snap it out of the air, he jumped up and began flapping his wings furiously.

It didn't work very well. He careened into some tall grass then plopped back down with a soft thud. His youthful enthusiasm was undaunted, however, and he continued to hop and flap. When they crested the hill, a gurgling brook came into view and Dragon saw the butterfly drink by putting its proboscis in the water. He submerged his snout in the stream and did the same.

"Now this is where the water enters the aqueduct," Kara said, pointing to a line of wooden troughs. "That's how running water is supplied to our

Sambuka Black

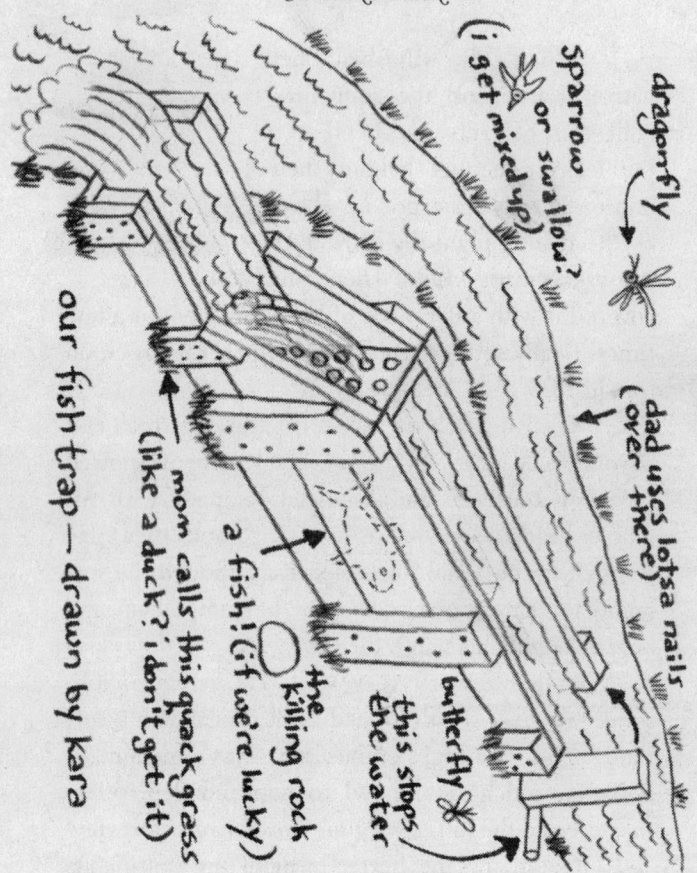

house, and this…" she walked a few steps and stopped next to a large wooden box, "is our fish trap. The water flows in here then out those little holes and back to the stream. And if we get lucky…Hey! We got one!"

They looked into the box and saw a large rainbow trout. Kara pushed a lever that closed the trough and all the water drained away, then she whacked the fish with a rock and lifted it out by the gills.

"Mmm, fish for dinner!"

They turned and started walking back down toward the house and Dragon kept jumping and fluttering till he spied a gliding sparrow. He spread his wings, got a running start, then drifted for quite a distance before coming to a rolling stop. Kara laughed and cheered at the valiant attempt and his almost graceful landing.

Reaching the bottom of the hill, she paused and sat down under an apple tree. Dragon hopped into her lap and nuzzled her neck.

"Everyone always said I was weird for wanting a dragon, but they were so wrong. You'd never hurt me, I know you wouldn't." He stretched out across her knobbly knees which were too thin to cradle him comfortably, but he didn't seem to care.

"I can't wait till you meet Gran. She's gonna love you. But she won't be too happy at first." Her brow furrowed as she studied his tiny spines and delicate looking wings. He looked up and wrinkled his brow ridges too.

"It'll be okay. Gran'll be on our side. Besides, other people have dragons! Like Ms. Wolke. She has the great big blue one that helps Dad sometimes. Maybe you could help Dad someday! And the butcher has red ones…but that's different… Once Mom and Dad meet you, once they see what you can do…like digging up grubs! That's my most important chore!"

Dragon chirped his agreement and jumped from her lap, leading the way back to the garden.

"Y'know, for being born yesterday, you learn awfully fast," Kara said as she followed. "Oh, hey! We have the same birthday!"

Dragon started peeping the Birthday Song while Kara giggled and hummed along.

"You're so smart! And you learned a word last night, too, I know you did. You said *cookie*." Dragon looked up.

Cookie!

"No, no, I don't have any," she said sheepishly. He inspected her upturned hands and sniffed the dangling fish, then recoiled from the aroma.

"Ho ho ho, that doesn't smell like a cookie does it? I'll get you one tonight, I promise. After we go see Gran."

Buzzing caught Kara's ear as a large beetle-like wasp zeroed in and she turned, hands flailing and terrified.

the wasp wasn't really this big but the buzzing was!

drawn by kara

Almost faster than she could see, Dragon streaked through the air, grabbed the beetle-wasp in his jaws and slammed it to the ground, crunching it and giving it a quick death shake, just for good measure.

"Whoa! That would've been *bad*!"

Dragon dropped the bug and looked up as if he was in trouble. Kara rushed over to reassure him.

"Good Dragon!" She snuggled him gratefully. "Very good Dragon! Dad always tells me to watch out for the wasps. They're so horrible! Good Dragon! And you flew! You flew for real!"

They spent the rest of the day together, feeding the chickens, playing hide and seek, sharing lunch. They read books about dragons and mythical creatures, and she threw a stick that he flew to fetch.

It might have gone on forever, but the sun was falling and Mom and Dad were due home soon. Kara took Dragon inside so they could get cleaned up while she contemplated the next step.

A Show at the Carnivale

Down the road from the village, set up in a small field, was a ragtag little circus of travel worn wonders. Brightly colored wagons ringed the edge of the clearing, carts with food and games were lined up in a long row, and flamboyant performers were wandering about, amusing onlookers with their tricks and acrobatics.

Splendid in his tatty velvet tailcoat, the grizzled barker enticed and beguiled, his rich exotic accent caressing the crowd. Elevated on his small stage, but dwarfed by the dazed red behind him, he posed and gestured. With its right forefoot, the huge dragon rotated a handle which turned the carnivale wheel and its six single-passenger buckets.

"Ladies! Gentlemen! And Ladies again. Approach at your own peril," announced the lascivious barker.

He pulled back the lips of the cloudy-eyed dragon to reveal its scary teeth.

Sambuka Black

A Show at the Carnivale

"Have you ever seen anything so menacing?" he taunted the onlookers in a growly tone.

"Oooooo!" they all gasped in unison.

He pushed the dragon's head toward the adjacent food cart and, *Whoosh!* flames shot out of its mouth searing strips of meat hanging from a rotisserie.

"Ahhhhh!" the crowd crooned.

"Have you ever seen anything so lethal? So terrifyingly strong?" The barker bent low to a group of pretty young women, "So virile?"

The women giggled and blushed.

"Well, honestly, he is a she…" he continued slyly, then with a big lusty smile, "But I am not!"

They giggled again and blushed even deeper. The barker straightened back up, posturing dramatically, and narrowed his eyes, "Now, which brave children will hazard a turn on the Wheel of Dooooom?!!"

Entering the fairground, Kara and her parents passed a group of small red dragons chained together at their necks, their wings trussed up behind them. A man with a stained leather apron was struggling to pull them along, obviously frustrated as they kept tangling their leads. Even though she was quite nervous, Kara was doing a pretty good job of hiding Dragon under the folds of her wrap.

"Can we say hi to Gran? Right away?" she asked, trying to be nonchalant.

"You know it's bad luck before the performance," said Mom, who then turned to Dad, "I'm not sure Nanna's act is appropriate for someone Kara's age."

"I think she's funny," said Kara, indignant.

"Yes, she certainly is that," conceded Mom, genuinely amused.

A willowy dark haired girl swung past overhead, catching Kara's eye. Dressed in a sparkly blue bodysuit adorned with tiny yellow feathers, and dangling from a long diaphanous sash, she whipped around a bendy spire, contorting and twisting and spinning as if she didn't know the ground was there to walk on.

"Say, isn't that little Yvette?" wondered Mom.

A Show at the Carnivale

Kara, utterly entranced, didn't hear and didn't notice that they had stopped in front of the Dragon-on-a-Stick cart.

Dad tapped her on the shoulder, "Hey Sweetheart, ya want an omelet? They're not dragons yet, just an egg."

She realized where they were standing, shook her head and backed away in disgust. Glancing between the food cart and the neighboring dart game trailer, she saw one of the small tethered reds lift its head and look at her alertly. She smiled and took a step forward.

Just then, the leash tightened and its head and neck were pulled out of sight. The shadow of a cleaver rose and fell and *CHUNK!* the dragon's body collapsed heavily.

Kara gasped in horror, pressed her hands protectively over her precious passenger and backpedaled, bumping hard into the elbow of a dart thrower. The dart went astray, glanced off a support post and arched skyward, hanging seemingly forever before dropping towards an unsuspecting victim. Dragon streaked from her vest, snatched the dart out of midair and

Sambuka Black

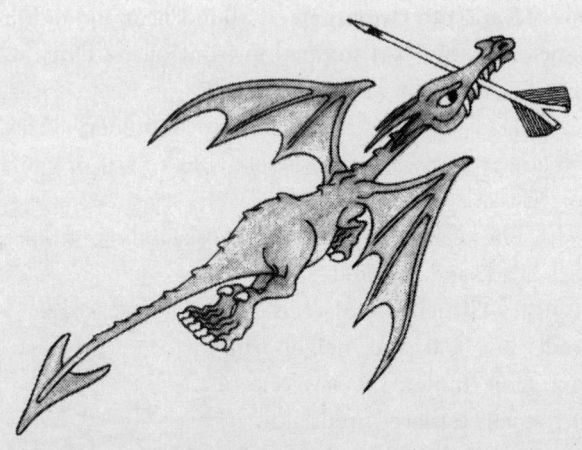

slammed it to the ground, then gave it a sharp killing shake.

He looked up, expecting praise.

The nearby crowd was aghast, then, realizing what they were looking at, fearfully enthralled by the sight of the unfettered purple dragon. Kara scooped him up and held him tight, trying desperately to keep a grip on her rising hysteria, but completely confused about what to do next.

"Kara, what have you done?" shouted Dad as he pushed through the excited crowd.

Mom was right behind him, "Put that thing down!"

A short distance away, Gran, in bizarre make-up, a hair net, and a thin robe over a skimpy

A Show at the Carnivale

costume, poked out of her tent to investigate the commotion. As she hurried toward her daughter's voice, she passed one of the frightened townsfolk running the other way.

The man raced through the cobbled town square and approached a pedestal displaying a patinated bronze statue of a tall, thin man holding a crystal ball. He nervously waved his hand over the weathered orb and it began to glow dimly.

Kara panicked and ran, not paying attention, and found herself behind the butcher cart. She tripped over something and fell, losing her grip on Dragon. Looking wildly about, she saw only bloody hanging meat quarters as he fluttered to the ground behind her.

Overhead, flames from the big dragon engulfed the roasting meat, illuminating the freshly beheaded corpse of the young red laying at her feet. Kara cowered, feeling sick, then saw Dragon and screamed, "RUN HOME!!"

Dragon, now frightened, started running and flying back to the house and, though the crowd was really just noisy, concerned and curious, Kara scrambled after him, terrified, her panic propelling her away from the angry mob.

Panting, she finally made it back home and called frantically for Dragon. He landed on her shoulder and curled around her neck, still fearful, though not sure why. The few members of the crowd actually in pursuit caught up, led by spunky Gran and distraught Mom and Dad.

"It was an accident! The bottle broke!" Kara desperately whispered to her grandmother.

"Oh dear girl," she replied. "Well, the cat's out of the bag now. I'm not sure what we should do." Kara's parents looked at Gran with raised eyebrows and open mouths.

The barker stepped forward, pushing his face close to Kara's, "That's a valuable little player you've got there. Very rare. I'll trade you my best red. Very tasty! Especially when very rare."

Kara backed away, "He's my friend! He's not for sale!"

Dad stepped between them, "Please stay back, my daughter's very upset."

"I'll make it two reds!" the barker raised.

Dad was more forceful, "I don't know what we're going to do. Please stay back!"

Mom tried to put her arm protectively around her daughter, but was obviously scared of Dragon, "Kara! Where did you get that, that thing?!"

"We need to go in!" she cried, pulling away toward the house.

"No, you can't take it inside! You shouldn't even be touching it!" Mom was mortified by the whole situation.

"I...You don't understand! It's okay! He's okay! He's smart! He's not just an animal!" Kara was trying desperately to get through to her parents, but they just weren't listening.

The small but boisterous crowd collected in the yard, chattering speculatively, when a huge blue dragon suddenly dropped out of the sky and landed in front of them. The spectators pulled back and fell silent when they realized who had arrived.

The tall thin man's hair was silver, short, and widows-peaked and he wore a long riding coat with gold buttons that shimmered in the light of the full moon. In one graceful motion, he dismounted, moving with the calm air of power.

The barker immediately approached, rambling sycophantically, "It's not one of ours, Minister James, Sir. We only have the reds! And all our eggs are accounted for. Of course we sent for you right away. And he's purple! Do you believe it? You don't see one of those everyday! Perhaps a small reward for such a find at my humble Carnivale?"

Ignoring the barker like a bug, the Minister stepped forward and did a quick, flowing hand gesture. Dragon sprang from Kara's shoulder, claws grazing her neck, and settled on his forearm, perched sullenly like a hooded falcon.

"Unrestrained dragons can be very dangerous, silly girl," lectured the Minister, spewing condescension. "It is fortunate I am here to relieve you of this vicious little thing. Those scratches are probably infected already." He turned on his heel and strode back toward his flyer.

Kara couldn't believe this was happening. "NO!!" she screamed, her face flushing crimson as she lunged, sobbing hysterically, and grabbed at his coat. He spun and yanked it away, glaring. Mom and Dad pulled Kara back, blanching under his intense gaze. Then, after a final, overly long glance at Gran, he smoothly mounted and flew away.

A Show at the Carnivale

Kara looked in her hand and realized it held a gold button. She clenched her fist around it in rage.

Gran tried to cam her down, "It's no use, dear. It's out of our control now."

"They're going to eat him!" she wailed.

"Now honey, we don't know that," Mom tried to console.

"If you really cared, you'd do something! Leave me alone!"

"Kara!" shouted Dad, bewildered, "Why are you behaving like this?!"

She wrestled away from them, screeching, "I hate you! I hate you all!" as she stormed into the house and slammed the door.

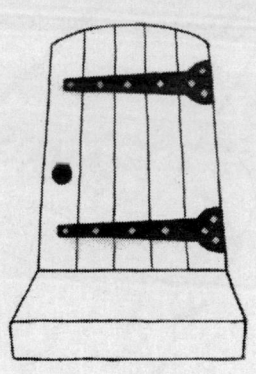

The Plan

The candle burned lower and lower as Kara fumed late, late into the night. Sitting at her desk with open books and papers, she mumbled to herself, "What's wrong with them? They don't care. They're just cowards. How can they be so stupid?"

From the very bottom of the bottom drawer, she lifted out her very oldest, very worn, leather bound book entitled,

and turned to a stained page which read,

Unbinding

Required Ingredients

I. Some thing of the enchantor

II. Some thing of the enchantee

III. Vaporizing agent, one drop

IV. Pinch of cyclops horn

V. Thimble of powdered blue coral

Kara looked up at the map on her wall, pausing to think, then picked up a piece of Dragon's eggshell. Her head tipped to the side as she studied it.

"Don't worry little one, I'll save you."

She may have slept on it, but Kara's face held as much determination in the morning brightness as it had in the candlelight of the night before. She was still lying in bed, but awake and waiting for her chance.

Dad opened the bedroom door and poked his head in to rouse her, "Morning Kara. Time to get up."

She didn't respond.

"Look, I know it feels like a big deal right now, but you'll see it's all for the best in the long run. I mean, could you see a full-grown dragon around here? Where would we have kept it? We couldn't have fed it," he implored, having practiced this speech all night.

"He could eat grubs!" Kara blurted out before she could stop herself.

"Come on, Kara, you're smarter than this! There is no way a dragon could exist on tiny little grubs. What about when it grew up? I'm sorry, it would just be too dangerous. Dragons don't belong in little girls' back yards. They're not pets!"

"He's not a pet! He's my friend!"

The Plan

Dad sighed. "Your mom and I have to go out. We need more cherry wood for the Gaudets' staircase. There's still leftover rabbit in the cooler chest and some fish from last night. And while we're gone, can you please take Mom's new bench over to the Garvers'?" He paused, then tenderly, "We'll talk some more about this tonight, okay?"

Receiving nothing but silence, he sighed again and closed the door.

A dark mutinous look crossed Kara's face. "That'll work," she growled, throwing back the covers.

She whipped her hooded cloak off the coat rack and stuffed it into her shoulder bag, the one her dad had woven years ago. She kept everything in that bag. This day, however, its usual contents had been unceremoniously heaped into a pile on the floor in the front room. Flinging aside string and shoes and games and tools, she waded through, snatching her knife, her compass, and her fire starter kit before tossing them in with the cloak, rope and hatchet.

Sambuka Black

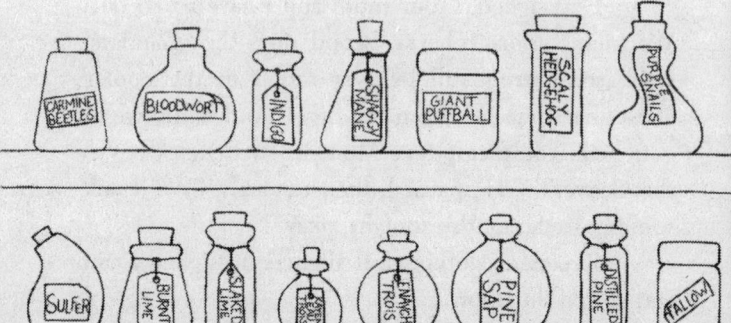

In Mom's workshop, she quickly scanned the little bottles on the shelf then grabbed one that read Kayen Eau Trois. In the kitchen, she bundled up the leftover rabbit and a loaf of bread and jammed them in with everything else.

Back upstairs, Kara added the spell book, her three copper coins and some clothes, then tried to charm the map into a small clear bottle. It only went in halfway. She tried a second time before giving up and just crammed it in the way it was.

Almost as an afterthought, she threw in her sketchbook, just for good measure, then paused,

The Plan

taking a last long look around her room.

She reached out to her copy of *A Dragon's Tale*, still sitting on the corner of her desk where Dad had left it, and opened it to the page where a pop-up image of a dragon unfolded. She turned a little silver hand crank and the dragon threw its head back, wailing at the night's sky. She was glad the book was not enchanted with sound because she knew her heart would have broken right then and there. After a long deep breath, she stole herself from her childhood haven.

The shoulder bag was heavy and unwieldy as Kara half dragged it down the stairs, so she tied it securely atop Mom's new bench. Sitting next to it, she yanked at the laces of the tough, knee high boots her grandfather had made. After six years, they were scuffed and stained but still fit as perfectly as ever.

"Come on, follow me. I need you more than the Garvers do right now." The bench rose a couple inches and trailed a few feet behind her.

She carefully led the way out the back door and through the garden so as not to be on the main road for very long. Staying to the edges and ready to

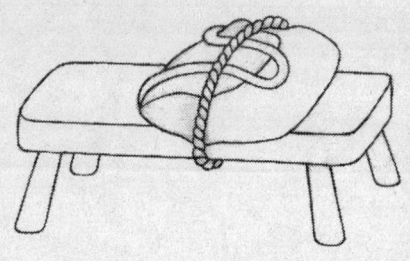

hide should anyone come by, she walked the gauntlet as quick as she could, knowing that the local bundles of sticks that passed for bushes didn't offer much cover.

Turning off the dusty potholed thoroughfare, she entered the woods on a small dirt path, barely wide enough for a single cart. At first, the vegetation seemed to be struggling, with dry looking trees and plants like those next to the road, but as she traveled farther in, the forest became more lush.

Around a bend, the path narrowed slightly, she stopped, reached into her bag and pulled out the map. She fanned out the part that was not in the bottle.

"We're here," she said, addressing the bench while pointing to a small dot labeled, Conway Springs, "and we need to go here."

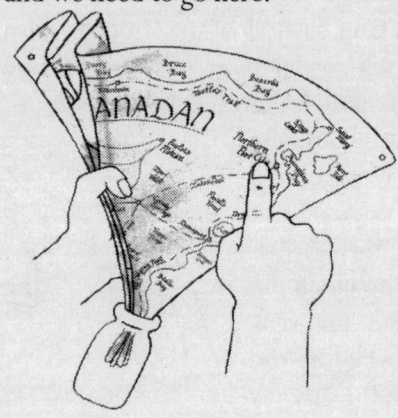

The Plan

Northern Port City was farther than Kara had ever been. She had heard stories, though. It was bustling with trade as it was located on a protected bay facing the Eastern Sea. Everyone knew that was where the Minister lived. His executive office was located in the rocky outcrop which overlooked the harbor so he could oversee all the goods that came and went.

At that very moment, the Minister happened to be looking out on his domain through an enormous window that filled an entire wall. Annoyed, he focused close in front of him and used a silk handkerchief to polish a small blemish on the thick, virtually smooth, but otherwise spotless, glass.

He turned at the sound of a wheeled cart.

"Ah, my new acquisition," he said, his eyes following a shroud of richly jeweled brocade which covered something about the size of a tall thin pumpkin. It came to a stop before him and the attending servant removed the cloth revealing a glass dome. Inside, a ten-inch tall human-like skeleton brandished a scimitar and shield and looked around with wild eyes. Realizing who was looking in, it smashed its shield against the glass which made the servant jump, the dome vibrate, and the Minister smile.

"Let's see. We need a nice pose," he intoned, amusement dancing in his voice as he leaned in close.

"Let him out."

The servant was shaky, but obediently removed the glass and jumped back. The skeleton lunged for the Minister's jugular but was instantly frozen.

"Yes, yes," the Minister's eyes twinkled, "very dramatic. This is an exceptional specimen."

The skeleton's eyes, however, were still shaking fiercely and it fixed him with a furious glare.

"These, however, are quite distracting." He plucked them out with a second wave of his hand and dropped them in a tall bottle where they joined a collection of other eyeballs floating in a sickly yellow liquid.

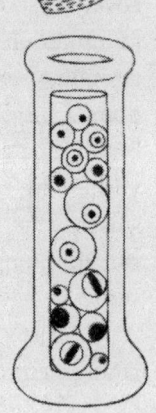

"Much better." He replaced the glass dome, but continued to examine his latest prize.

"Will that be all, sir?" asked the servant hesitantly.

The Plan

"There is a business of bobbykins in the West Territory. They need to be eradicated. Use the concentrated mercury waste from the sewage filter to contaminate their water supply."

"Yes Minister."

"The dragons in the lower foundry are consuming too much food, cut their rations. I should see their ribs."

"Yes Minister."

The Minister picked up the skeleton-under-glass, "And you, my treasure, deserve a place of honor."

The servant started to wheel the cart away but stopped, attentive, when the Minister spoke again.

"The cleaning servant who did the windows is lacking. Have her children put in the mines for a week."

"Y-yes Minister."

"Perhaps that will help her focus on the job at hand," he finished, turning his back in dismissal.

Mythical Creatures

Still pointing at the map, Kara continued, "It's about fifty miles, but we need to stay away from the road so no one will see us."

She stuffed the map/bottle back into her bag and started down the path again, her wooden companion floating beside her. After a while, the path got narrower and she got tired, so she pulled out her spell book and climbed onto the bench. It lowered a bit under her weight and moved slightly slower, but other than an occasional bumpy patch, she could ride and read at the same time.

She let out a deep worried sigh, "...I have a piece of Dragon's eggshell, the button, and the vaporizer, but where am I going to find cyclops horn? What am I gonna use for that?!"

The path had become almost non-existent as they traveled through some grasslands and Kara had

Mythical Creatures

fallen asleep on the bench, the easy motion of smooth terrain lulling her into a doze. The grass had turned back to trees when she woke with a start and tumbled partly off, disoriented. "Mom? Dad?"

She heard screaming and snarling and rustling leaves, then running footsteps passed nearby and quickly faded. After a quiet moment, there was a sharp cry followed by growling and grunting and breaking branches. Crossing the path behind her, a purple satyr ran for her life, a huge, muscley, four-armed cyclops lumbering behind.

Out of the corner of her eye, Kara caught a flash of color and spun, terrified, then finally saw the creatures as the cyclops pounced and took the small satyr to the ground. He held her hands over her head with his upper arms, opened his jaws wide and viciously closed them on her throat.

Unable to look away, Kara stood with her knuckles stuffed in her mouth.

Sambuka Black

With his lower hands, Duncan tickled Alex's bare ribs while she laughed and squealed. They rolled and Alex was on top staring at Kara staring at them. Kara gasped.

"Oh! Uh, hi! We were just…playing," Alex stammered, getting up.

Duncan, clad in a knee-length kilt and looking around frantically, jumped up, grabbed Alex and pulled her behind him with one hand, then drew his machete, axe and knife with the other three.

Kara pointed at Alex, "You're naked."

"Are you alone?!" Duncan demanded.

"You're NAKED!" Kara said again.

"ARE YOU ALONE!!!" Duncan roared, brandishing his weapons.

Kara suddenly snapped to and cowered behind a nearby tree.

Alex stepped around Duncan with mild annoyance, waving him back a little. Kara peeked out and saw the faun woman raise her hand up next to a tree limb.

"A favor little ones?" she said. A column of fuzzy pink caterpillars came marching down her arm, crossed rippled scars that splashed across her upper back, then settled themselves around her torso into a nice, fashionable, form-fitting top.

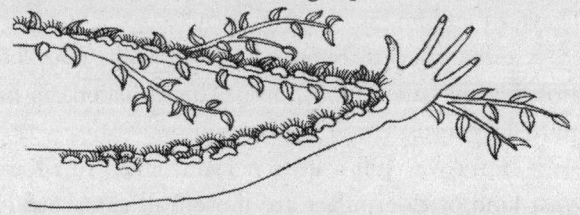

"It's okay little puppy, you can come out. We're not going to hurt you or anything."

Kara cautiously came out from behind the tree.

Alex stepped toward her, "Are you out here all by yourself?"

Kara was emboldened now that Alex was no longer topless and Duncan had calmed down somewhat. "I'm on a mission," she stated, determination returning to her voice, "A friend of mine has been captured."

"Captured?!" repeated Alex. Her cat-like ears twitched nervously and her little white tail flicked back and forth.

"He's a dragon. The Minister took him."

This did nothing to soothe Alex and she tried to hide the worried look that passed between her and Duncan. "Oh. That's very bad," she said, again focused on Kara. "What about your parents? Do they know?"

Kara's rage from the night before came bubbling up all over again. "Yes! And they don't care! They just let him take Dragon away!"

Alex tried to be comforting, "Well, that was probably the safest thing to do. The Minister can be quite dangerous. Um, I'm Alex."

Kara was still a little nervous and, "I'm Kara what kind of caterpillars are those?" all came out in one quick sentence.

"I don't know, but they're wonderful. Always willing to help," she replied with a smile.

Kara put her face close, intently studying the beautiful insects. "They're pink!"

"Uh, yes they are," Alex agreed, "and th-"

"And your pupils are rectangular. They're beautiful!"

"Why, thank you. And the big scary guy over there is Duncan."

Kara looked up and cocked her head, then

asked, "Were you afraid of me?"

"No! No, not just you, alone, by yourself," Duncan sputtered. "Most humans…aren't very kind…to our kind."

"Huh, they told me you weren't even real," she said, mostly to herself, then, "Are there more of you?"

"Not as many as there used to be," Alex said sardonically. "I mean, no, not here, not right now."

"My Gran used to tell me stories about the colorful people who lived in the forest."

"Sadly, no one calls us colorful people anymore. The few humans who do know we exist, mostly just fear us." Alex's face was sad, too, and she suddenly looked much older.

Duncan, however, became more agitated, "There is some evidence we're hunted for sport and even sold for meat."

"Here we go…" said Alex, rolling her eyes.

"They eat infant dragons! Why not us? Some say the Minister shrinks down our heads and wears them like jewelry! Truthiness can be stranger than reality!" He was emoting theatrically, weapons still in hand.

"Stop exaggerating now," Alex said, trying to force a smile. "And put those things away, you'll traumatize the poor girl!"

Though conflicted, Duncan forced himself to

be less intimidating. "Um, so, do you know where you're going? Do you have a plan?" he asked while returning his accoutrements to their places on his belt.

"Yes!" said Kara excitedly, "I have a map!" She pulled it out, but then got embarrassed when she realized the half-in/half-out-map-in-a-bottle looked a little pathetic. She stuffed it back in her bag.

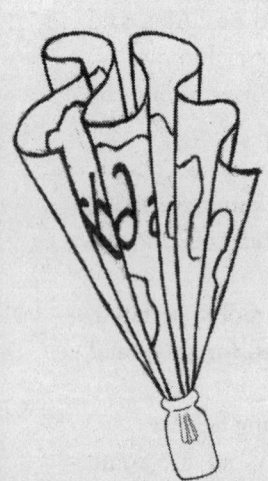

"And…and a spell! I mean, a recipe for a spell…" she fumbled through her things. "I have this book! I need some blue coral, and some powdered sahhh…" she trailed off, mouth agape, staring at the horn protruding from Duncan's forehead.

Alex noticed her hesitation and decided to intervene. "Ya know, it's going to be dark soon and we live just over there a ways. Are you hungry, do you want some dinner?"

"I don't eat dragon!" Kara blurted out.

"Good heavens no! Some of our best friends are dragons. But we do eat…" she glanced about for something on the ground, "dragon food!" She held up a jar of squiggling grubs.

Mythical Creatures

"I knew it! I knew dragons could live on grubs." Kara paused. "You eat grubs?!"

"We love cooking with grubs!" Duncan exclaimed with relish, "Grub casseroles, grub broth, grub pies...!"

"And my specialty, grub & mushroom vermicelli!" Alex inserted, "A little garlic, a little butter, a little basil...it's all in the preparation."

"And of course when I say we, I mean Miss Alex. She's really talented with the filleting and the sautéing and the fonduing and the meuniering and the demi-glacing and...Oh, who's this?" Duncan squatted down by the floating bench.

"It's a bench."

"What's its name?" he asked.

"Uh, it doesn't have a name. It's a bench."

"We could give it a name," Duncan suggested as they walked off into the woods.

The trio approached an enormous tree. Alex and Kara were walking in front, followed by Duncan and the bench.

"...strawberry mustaches!" Duncan was

saying, "Bring a bag of those to a party and you'll be the talk of the town!"

"Duncan! Stop it!" Alex scolded, smiling, then in response to Kara's mystified expression, "These caterpillars have an unusual defense mechanism. Anything, or anyone, who tries to mess with them gets all giddy and euphoric. Duncan here figured out if you scare 'em, you know, roar at them really loud or something," she gave him a sideways look, "they'll do their thing."

Duncan bowed his head sheepishly, but couldn't help letting out a giggle before catching himself.

"So, can you talk to grubs, too?" Kara asked.

"Oh! There's no talking to them," Alex said, waving her hand in disgust. Just then they were greeted by a bob tailed, short hair tabby cat. It sat on its haunches and stretched up as if asking for a hug.

Kara bent down to pet it, "Who's this?"

"That's Paul!" Duncan said, "She lives under the tree."

"Paul?" she laughed, "That's not a cat's name. That's a person's name."

"Oh." He paused, brow pondering, "What would you call her?" he asked humbly.

"I don't know. Fluffy? Mittens? Bugsy?" she suggested, trying to be helpful.

Stroking his goatee thoughtfully, Duncan

Mythical Creatures

drifted off, trying out the name "Bugsy" with different inflections.

"Bugsy. *Bug*-sy. Bug-*sy*. Bugsy lives under the tree..." he rhymed, getting into a sing-song rhythm.

Kara turned back to Alex, "And where do you live?"

They rounded the huge trunk, and she saw two windows, a chimney, and steps that led up to a door crowned with a sign that read Chez Champignon.

"*In* the tree!" Alex announced.

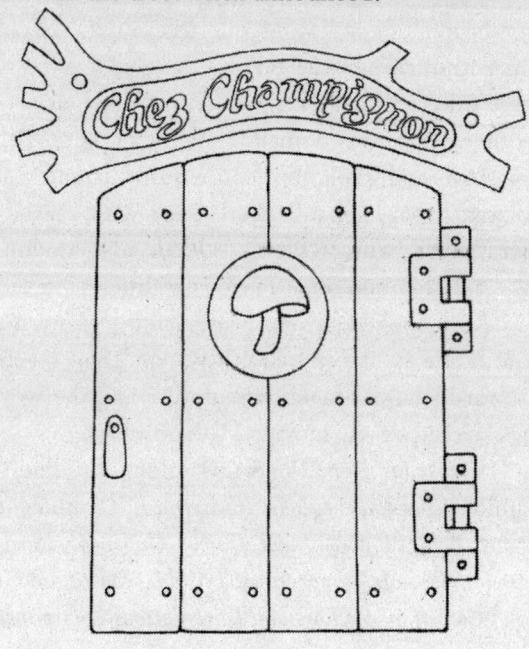

The Real Story

Inside the hollowed out tree was a circular room with furniture carved into the tree itself, a bed on one side, a table and two different sized chairs on the other. There was a small kitchen complete with a brick stove and cook top, and a stone counter and sink next to it. The walls were lined with carved in shelves overflowing with an eclectic assortment of books, artwork and other curious oddities.

Kara looked around, fascinated. "Wow. Your whole house is like my Gran's wagon." She reached up toward a large dragonfly sculpture and the woven wings started slowly moving by themselves.

She ran her fingertips along a line of unfamiliar books, *Legends of Mythical Creatures, The Dragons' Book of Myths and Secrets, Under My Spell-A Manifesto, Downfall-Coppers and Golds, David and the Keys of Catastrophe, Claws and Lamentations, A Fire Inside,*

The Real Story

Karma Shastra, *Where the Cobblestones End-A Collection of Dragon Poetry*, *Insects-Exotic and Mundane*, *Keeping Dirt Alive*, *Soothing the Mandrake*, and *Cyclops Whisperer*. The last title looked especially worn.

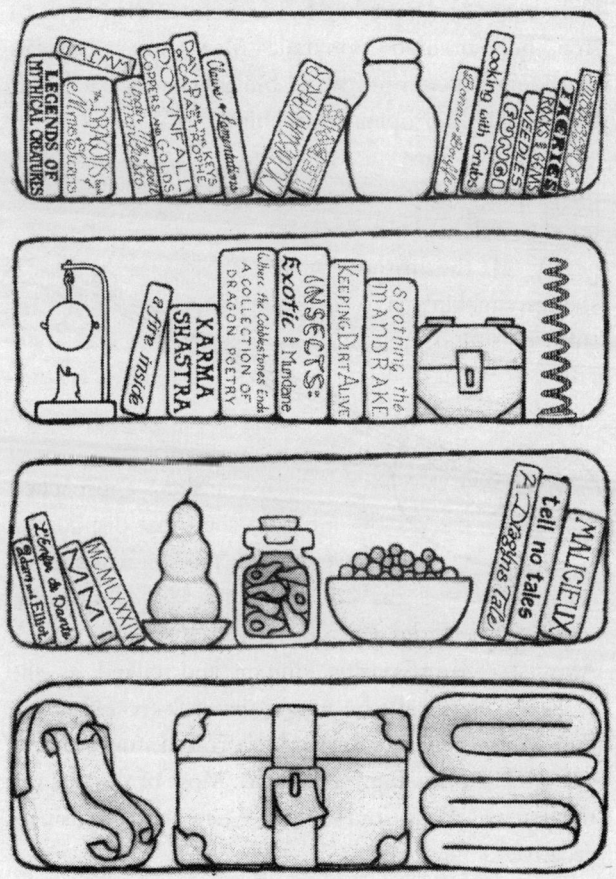

Alex was by a small window, her arm extended outside to some nearby foliage. "Thank you my darlings," she crooned as the caterpillars filed out. She pulled a stylish short sleeved shirt past her nubby little horns and over her head, then reached back to free her braided ponytail. Meanwhile, Duncan considered the empty wood bin then went back out, leaving the door open behind him.

Kara saw a beautiful purpleheart mandoré hanging on the wall and plucked gently at the catgut strings, making a soft rich sound.

She approached a shelf that displayed a twenty inch tall spiral sculpture carved out of a piece of zebrawood.

"Where did you get all this stuff?" she asked. Alex started preparing dinner and talked as she worked. "Well, all the magic things were gifts. Oh, that one's s'posed to have a little round stone with it, but it's been missing for months. Most of the rest are things we made ourselves. We're embarrassingly creative."

The Real Story

Kara bent down and slid a book partway out from a lower shelf, discovering a round polished stone balanced on top of the pages between the covers. She placed it in a divot at the base of the spiral and it began rolling to the top then back down again. She marveled at its simple hypnotic beauty.

"Hey! Good eyes! Duncan will be very happy about that," Alex called from the cooking area.

"Hey, I have this book," Kara called back, pulling out another very worn leather bound tome entitled, *A Dragyn's Tale*. "But mine's different."

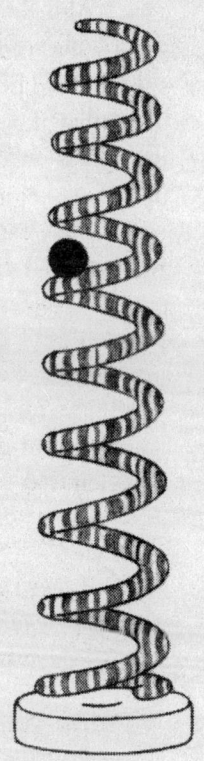

The book in her hands was smaller and when she opened it, there were no pop up pictures and no little hand cranks. Instead, the flat painted images moved slightly, illustrating the story.

"The ending's different too, I bet," Alex scoffed. "Let me guess, in yours the wizard defeats the dragon."

"Mm-hm," Kara nodded with disgust.

Alex wiped her hands on a towel and walked

over, "Well, in this version, the dragon just left the wizard covered in mud. He made friends with the villagers and became quite well known. Some people think that if you re-write history, it makes it true. But this is an original handmade first edition. It has the whole beginning part, too. Look."

They sat, opened the book to the beginning, and watched the colorful paintings play across the pages.

> *In an elaborately decorated room of marble and tapestries, a young boy, resplendent in opulent golden robes and a red silk turban, watches a dragon egg as its pearlescent mint colored shell cracks.*
>
> *A puppyish, wingless, green dragon jumps on the giggling Prince and licks his face with a long forked tongue.*
>
> *The teenage Prince and his indulgent father, the Sultan, feed and pet the now wagon-sized dragon who preens, its wings out and head held high, a ruby studded harness across its chest.*
>
> *The Prince and the dragon run through the palace playing hide and seek, smiling and laughing.*

The Real Story

The Prince jumps from an alcove, startling the dragon who belches fire, badly burning his friend.

The next image made Kara gulp. The dragon's reaction covered such a gamut of emotions from shock to realization to grief, that her eyes filled with tears. She dabbed them with her sleeve as Alex turned another page.

The Prince lies in bed, bandages covering much of his body including one side of his face, the dragon's nose nuzzling his hand, the Sultan sitting beside them.

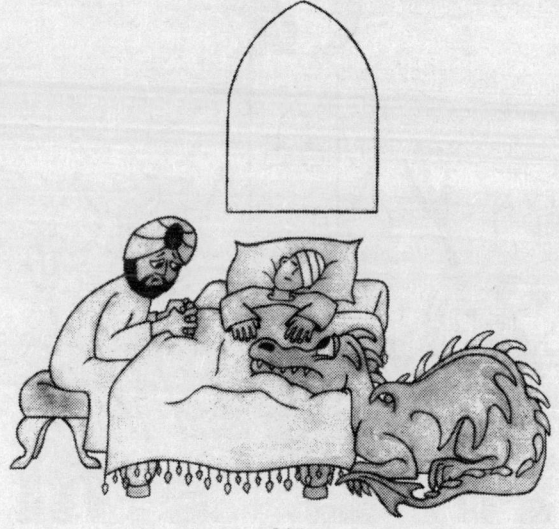

Sambuka Black

On the grounds below, the angry citizens are rioting, pitchforks and torches held aloft, crying for the dragon's head.

With watery eyes, the Sultan hugs the guilt ridden dragon, but must send him away.

The dragon flies through the night, past the full moon, settles on a mountaintop and, heart broken, throws his head back, wailing at the sky.

"I always wondered why he was crying," Kara said softly.

"The Sultan told him the townspeople would never listen to reason and that he could never return. He must have felt so alone," Alex trailed off, her eyes glistening as well.

"It's so sad!" said Kara.

"What's really sad is that Prince Silas came looking for him, but he was already gone."

"Did he find him?!

"No. He searched for many years but they...they never saw each other again." After a melancholy moment, Alex changed the subject.

"So, what about your parents?" she asked, returning to dinner preparations.

"My dad's an architect! He builds these really amazing houses with stained glass skylights, slider stairs, aperture windows, spiral elevators..." Kara paused, trying to remember more details.

"Elevators?" queried Alex.

"Yeah, like a mechanical platform that lifts you to the top of the house."

"Oh. Huh. Um, actually, I meant what's their magic?" Just then, Duncan came up the steps and started backing into the house with armloads of firewood.

Kara smiled devilishly, "My mom says men get the power to carry things for us." Alex threw her head back and laughed out loud. Duncan, eager to be in on the joke, quickly turned and slammed his horn into the doorframe.

"Aw, fuh cryin' out loud!" he cursed himself.

With a pained smile, Alex tentatively waved her fingers at him, "Hey babe," then whispered to Kara, "They can be kinda clumsy, though." The girls grinned guiltily at each other.

Duncan dropped logs in their bin then smacked the end of a wooden dowel and used it to light a pile of kindling in the stove, all the while grumbling to himself, "Stupid horn! I outta chop you off! How 'bout that? I'll grind ya down to a little bump. Always in the way stupid good for nuthin' piece of---Oh, hey, the ball's back!"

Alex drowned him out, announcing simply, "I like his horn."

Kara concurred, "I think he's keeping it."

Duncan, massaging his skull, pulled up a sturdy wooden stool and joined them at the table, "I'm such a bonehead."

"But such a cute bonehead," retorted Alex as she squeezed his arm lovingly, "and he's really talented and industrious. Why, in one summer, he hollowed out this whole tree and made our home, not to mention carving that beautiful banderole above the door."

Kara said brightly, "I carve chains."

"Oooo, nice!" Duncan exclaimed, "I've seen those. Very difficult. You must have a lot of patience!"

"Well, I only do a little at a time. It takes forever!"

"Are they magic chains?" asked Alex.

"No," she replied shyly, "they just start out as a solid piece of wood."

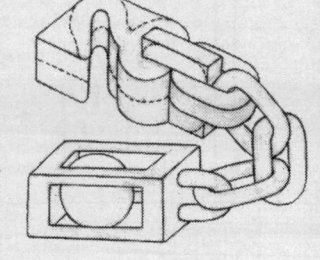

"Oh. I'm sorry. I didn't mean to imply, that without…"

"It's okay. I don't have my magic yet. My mom says I'm just a late bloomer," but then she brightened, "I can carve a ball inside a cage, too."

"Wow, you're kind of embarrassingly creative, yourself! Hey, come look at this." Alex retrieved a small contraption consisting of a hammered copper sphere hanging from a miniature gallows. She unhooked the dangling ball and held it in a pot of water where it gurgled as small bubbles escaped from one of two curved tubes protruding from opposite sides. After a few seconds, she pulled it back out and gave it a shake.

"That sounds like enough," she said, satisfied.

She hung it back up, stepped to the wood stove and pulled out a burning twig then lit a candle sitting under the suspended sphere. She rested her elbows on the counter, chin in hands, staring at it.

Sambuka Black

Kara did the same.

After a moment, Alex turned and said, "Actually, nothing really happens for a few minutes. And what's your mom's power?"

"She builds furniture that can move by itself. You know, for redecorating."

"So that's why Buddy floats behind you?" asked Duncan.

"Buddy?"

"Your bench."

"Oh…yeah," she said, realizing what he was talking about. "Ya just tell it where to go. And my mom can carve, too. She's really good at vines and flowers and stuff like that, and she used to make the most amazing things but she says most people can't really afford fancy things these days."

"Yeah," Alex sighed, "and a few have way more than they deserve. But you know, a wise woman once told me, 'Enough is as much as a feast'."

The metal ball started to whine. They looked over and saw it spinning madly, steam shooting out of each of the curved tubes.

Kara's face twisted in thought, "Sooo…then,

that's steam!" she declared, wondrous recognition dawning on her face. "It's not magic at all!"

"Nope!" Alex smiled like she had just played a joke. Kara giggled.

"Now, you said you don't have your magic yet?" Alex asked. "Did you mean both talents? Don't all girls get something from their mom's mom?"

"Oh. Yeah." Kara was a little embarrassed, but figured she should explain. "My mom can change her eye color, just like her grandmother. And my Gran can put things in bottles. I can too, but," she paused, "I'm not very good. I don't practice enough."

Duncan was very intrigued, "Will you show us?"

Kara hesitated, "Oh, I don't know…"

"Pleeeeeease…?" pleaded Duncan and Alex.

"Okay. I'll try," she agreed half heartedly.

She poured her map out onto the table and pointed the bottle, staring hard. The map still only made it halfway back in. Flushing a deep red, she tried again, concentrating intently by scrunching up her face and closing her eyes.

The bottle began to vibrate but instead of drawing in the parchment, it suddenly jerked her forward then escaped her grip, sucking in Duncan's forearm.

He jumped up and away from the table, traumatized by the sight of his tiny hand sprouting

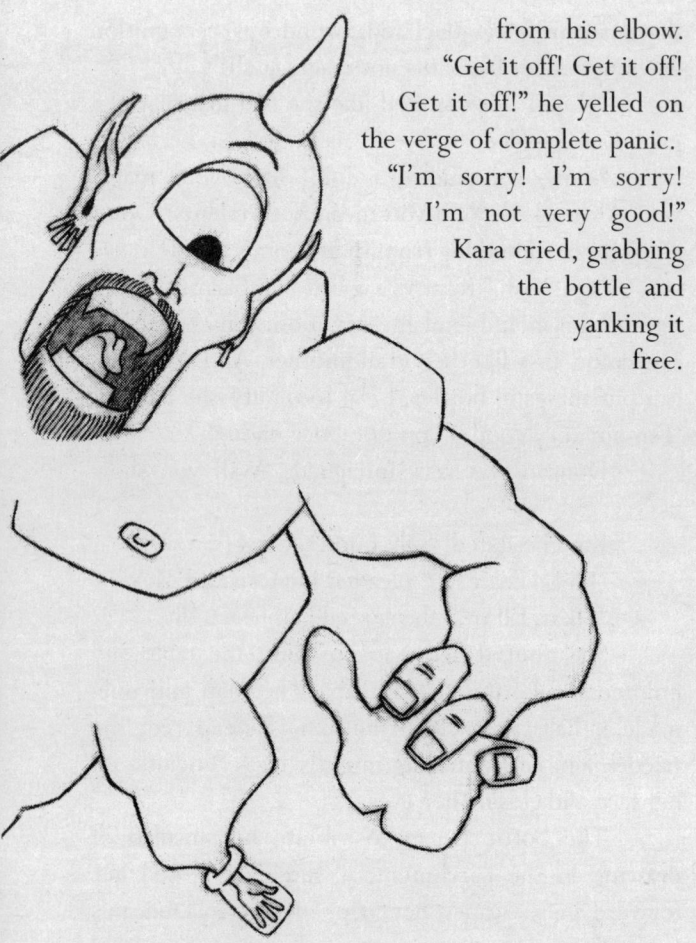

from his elbow. "Get it off! Get it off! Get it off!" he yelled on the verge of complete panic. "I'm sorry! I'm sorry! I'm not very good!" Kara cried, grabbing the bottle and yanking it free.

The obviously distraught Duncan flexed his fingers as Alex tried to calm him.

The Real Story

Kara tried to help, too. "It's okay! Your arm wasn't really small!" She gestured to the bottle. "It's bigger on the inside! Like my dad's houses!" She was almost in tears. "That's his magic," she continued, taking deep breaths, "his houses are bigger on the inside than on the outside."

"Oh, hey, I'm sorry," apologized Duncan, "I didn't mean to scare you. I just…I…" he faltered.

Alex continued for him, but haltingly, "Um, Duncan and I had a really bad experience a few years ago. We lost a good friend of ours."

Kara was still blinking back tears, "Lost? Did he die?"

Alex glanced at Duncan. "Wow. We haven't talked about this in a long time." She swallowed hard, touching a small doeskin pouch tied at her neck. "This one day, when we were still just kids really, we were hiking in the mountains and…"

Sexapus

Thump! Thump! Thump! Duncan hopped down the rough mountain trail on his calloused left foot as errant rays of sunlight scattered through the snow-dusted foliage. "Ow! Ow! Ow!" he wailed as he bobbed up and down, his stubbed right toes cradled protectively in his lower hands. "That's not what I meant to do!"

"But you're so good at it," smirked Alex as she trotted ahead on her perfectly pedicured purple hooves.

Kyle's own four thick legs moved with surprising grace as they easily carried his bulk. *And with only two feet no less*, his deep baritone chuckled.

Sexapus

He gently swayed as he threaded his way through the crowding trees, his great wings folded smoothly against his back to avoid low hanging branches.

Smiling broadly, Duncan turned and, hopping backward, taunted the huge dragon with, "Hey Kyle! 'Member that time I dared you to spook those trolls? Ya scared 'em right outa their loincloths!"

I remember. The sight of those lumpy hairy buttocks bouncing off into the woods...

A low chortle began rumbling inside Duncan.

...has scarred me for life. Kyle's reproachful tone caused Duncan's laughter to erupt.

I have nightmares still because of your silly challenge.

"Well, that's just the kind of thing friends do for each other." He gave Kyle three playful punches to the shoulder.

Grinning, Kyle playfully punched him back, and Duncan was launched into the bushes with much crashing and exclaiming.

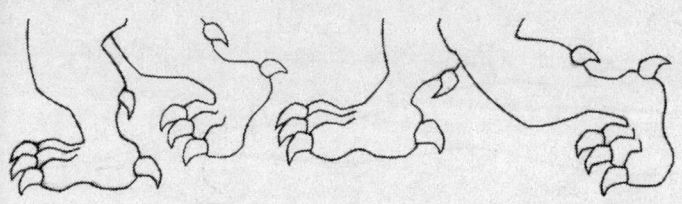

Alex, trying to ignore the shenanigans, rolled her eyes as she pulled her soft fur cape tighter about her shoulders to ward off the chilly morning air. "Well, *I* remember two friends who serenaded those odious trolls for *weeks* before they were forgiven."

Duncan popped back onto the trail like nothing had happened and brushed brambles from his knee length pants as Alex added, "Hey guys, I'm not seeing any more footprints…"

"Oh! Oh! And remember when we were kids and I walked across that rickety old suspension bridge? And I did it on my hands?!"

"Wow, a feat for the ages, Mr. Octopus," chided Alex, warm sarcasm seeping through.

"And it was pitch black!" bragged Duncan. "It's the most loftiest thing I ever did!" He puffed out his narrow chest and proudly stroked his newly sprouted whiskers before wrinkling his brow in thought, "And I only have *six* arms." He looked down just to make sure.

"Fine," said Alex with an exasperated grin, "Six-a-pus then!"

"Sexapus, eh? I like it!" Duncan started strutting and snapping his fingers, off in his own tavern-entertainer world, "Hey baby, I'm a sexapus!"

"No! Wait! I didn't…I meant…I said *SIX*-a-puss!" insisted Alex, flustered. "Yeah? Oh yeah?! Well, what do Duncan the Sexapus and Oswald the Oblivious have in common?" she demanded over her shoulder as she pushed through some overgrown bushes. Duncan and Kyle shrugged.

"They both have the…"

Alex gasped as she stepped out into a clearing. Her friends came up on either side and they all fell silent, gazing out over a stunning landscape. Several yards ahead a sharp drop off gave way to a sparkling carpet of frosted trees far below.

"…same middle name," Alex lamely finished her joke.

Duncan laughed out loud, a little too forcefully to be genuine.

Kyle started chuckling, *Heh heh heh, same middle name. Good one Miss Alex.*

Duncan's laughing had run down to a puzzled expression. He leaned over Alex's head and whispered to Kyle, "I don't get it."

"Hey look, under that old tree!" Alex scampered across the rocky icy surface to stand near the edge of the cliff. Duncan, arms outstretched, quickly followed like a parent overly concerned about his wobbly toddler.

"Alex! Be careful! It looks slippery!"

Kyle stepped forward as well, *I have to agree, Miss Alex, it does look a bit precarious.*

"Oh relax, I'm fine." She waved them off dismissively but, just in case, placed a cautious hand on one of the low branches. She kicked at the snow covered remnants of a campfire, "See? This is only a couple days old. He was here, I know it!"

Behind the trio, a tall young man with flowing blond hair, dressed in leather pants, a long open riding coat and a wide brimmed hat, hurled a giant fireball toward Duncan.

Kyle saw it just in time and threw a wing around his friends, but the force of the blast tumbled them all off the cliff.

With four of his arms, Duncan seized the tree trunk, his other two encircling the tail of falling Kyle who, in one motion, used his teeth to snatch Alex by her ponytail and fling her upward as the tree lurched violently, threatening its tenuous grip on the cliff's edge. Alex landed in a heap back on solid ground but was immediately jerked sideways as she screamed for Duncan.

Duncan's fingers dug into rotting bark and two of his nails tore out as he hung on for dear life

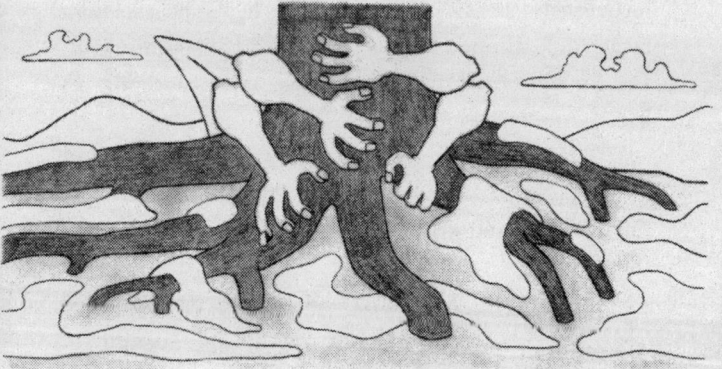

while Kyle desperately scrambled backwards, his claws finding no purchase on the sheer rock face. He instinctively flapped his powerful wings but his right was tattered and charred and he only succeeded in swinging and spinning, his twisting tail ridges scraping the flesh of Duncan's crumbling embrace. A root snapped, then another, and a shower of dirt and stones fell away toward the river that raged hundreds of feet below.

Duncan! LET GO! The tree was almost loose. Duncan's face was contorted in horror as Kyle roared inside his head, *SAVE ALEX!!*

He released his friend and clambered up without looking back. He broke off a gnarled branch, grabbed a chunk of rock and pulled out his machete, axe, whip and knife.

The blond man casually dragged the ferociously struggling Alex by her hair. She ran up a large rock, flipped into an awkward back somersault and kicked out, breaking his nose and dislodging his hat.

She pulled free and started to bound away, but he stretched out a clutching hand and invisible fingers wrapped around her throat and lifted her off the ground.

Writhing in agony, she floated back toward him while he turned to watch for the cyclops.

A small trickle of blood ran from his nose as he carefully replaced his hat.

Duncan leapt over a craggy boulder sweating and snorting like

Sexapus

a mad bull but froze when he saw Alex suspended in midair.

The young Mr. James spoke in a soft controlled voice, "You don't want your little friend to experience any more discomfort."

Alex convulsed and let out a strangled whimper. Duncan was shaking with fury, but helpless.

"I want two of your arms," the thin man stated.

Duncan growled yet without hesitation raised his machete.

"Not like that," commanded the future Minister as he gestured with his other hand. It was Duncan's turn to scream as his two lower arms began to warp and shrink and their bones kinked and shattered. Simultaneously, the wizard's shoulders shuddered and expanded under his long coat.

Satisfied, he quickly turned and was gone.

Duncan collapsed to his knees as Alex dropped and once again slammed hard against the ground. She crawled to him as he continued to painfully spasm.

"Your arms!"

"I guess I'm not your sexapus anymore," he gritted through clenched teeth.

"KYLE?!"

Duncan shook and began to weep.

Alex wrapped her arms around his huge head, her staring eyes haunted and glistening.

Two hours later and ten miles east of the river, the ambitious and calculating young wizard held aloft a small crystal ball as he spoke, "There has been a delay. I shall arrive in one week's time."

He returned the crystal to an inside pocket and tried to get comfortable on the rough green hide beneath him. The dragon's eyes were cloudy and gray instead of their usual, bright sparkling yellow and he lumbered on, mechanical and mindless.

"You will do as you're told Kyle. You will not be brave at the foundry," directed the man, studying and flexing his new hands, proud of his accomplishment.

The bright afternoon sunlight was melting the snow as Duncan and Alex slogged through the slush along the muddy embankment, she on his shoulders, scanning their surroundings, "Still no sign of him."

"It's been two weeks now," Duncan said wearily.

"We can't give up," Alex insisted. "If he was…dead…we would have found his body by now. If only I hadn't made us climb that stupid mountain!" Her self-loathing trailed off to a private rant inside her own head.

"Alex, it's not your fault," Duncan said softly. "You didn't make us do anything. We all wanted to find him."

"We have to keep looking!"

"We will, I promise. Even if it takes us all the way to the Northern Sea." They determinedly trudged on, Duncan staring into the distance as Alex started to whistle a lament, slow and somber.

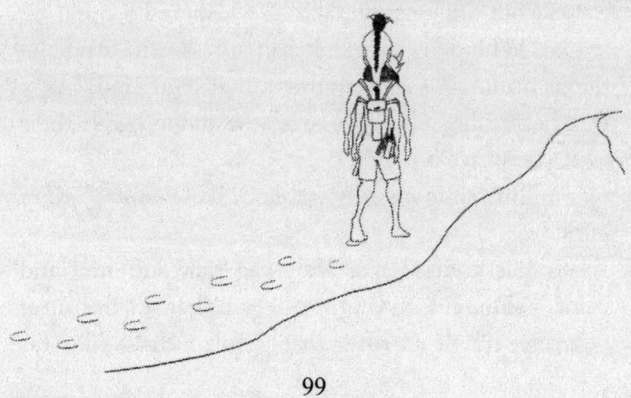

Dinner

"We finally found him in the port city," Alex continued. "He didn't even know we were there. Thanks to Minister James, almost all the dragons are like that now."

"But dragons can talk…" whispered Kara.

"Whipped, worked half to death. And he thinks nothing of feeding them their own kind!" Alex was beside herself. "The sick, the dying, even their own young are butchered-"

"But dragons CAN talk! Like people!" Kara burst in.

"Of course! Yes. They can talk and sing and paint," she said, trying to regain her composure, pointing, "Kyle wrote that book. That was his

Dinner

childhood. He burned his best friend, then he...he..." She couldn't continue. Kara's mouth moved, but nothing came out.

Alex took a deep breath, "Okay...I think it's time for dinner." She stood up and moved back to the cooking area.

"You were all looking for the Prince!" Kara exclaimed.

Duncan nodded, "But we didn't find him for years, and then it was too late."

"So you couldn't save Kyle?"

"We tried, many times," he said, his tone subdued. "We could break his chains, but we couldn't break the spell."

"But you, maybe, you're human," Alex interjected. "You have magic. I mean...for your friend. If you don't try to save him, you'll never forgive yourself." Shaken, she turned her head and returned to her chopping, whistling a downtrodden yet fierce tune.

"Couldn't you drag him away?" Kara asked Duncan.

"It's not so easy to move a two ton dragon. He's still there, still a slave, turning wheels and blowing fire on the boilers.

"Like the carnivale dragon," Kara said softly.

"That's why we built our house here, to be close. We used to go see him a lot, but it just got too hard." He gestured in Alex's direction and lowered his voice, "She would cry for days after each visit. Kyle wouldn't want that."

"But if my spell works! Then, maybe…"

"Um, let's not say that out loud," he glanced toward the kitchen, "we don't want to get Alex's hopes up too much. For now, we should just worry about your little friend. C'mon, let's clear the table for her."

Kara tried to enchant her map back into the bottle and this time, after a couple attempts, was able to get it all the way inside. Duncan smiled broadly and clapped all his hands in congratulations.

When dinner was ready, Alex presented Duncan and Kara each a plate of food that looked like a piece of art. Duncan's serving was about five

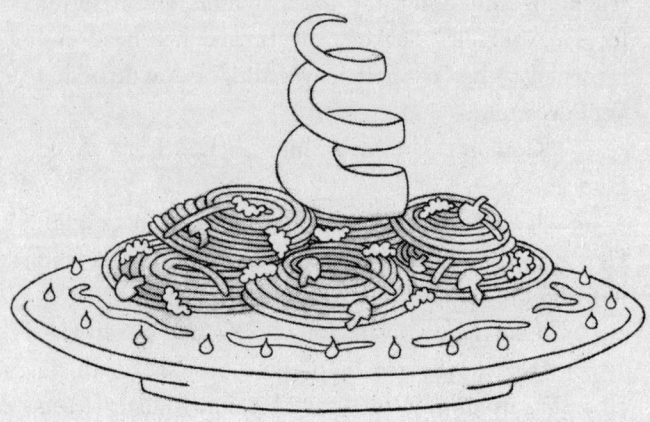

Dinner

times bigger, but other than that, they were identical. Neatly arranged noodles peppered with brightly colored juicy bits and garnished with a crunchy, sparkly curlicue of something blue. Having only two plates and two forks, Alex ate out of the pot with chopsticks.

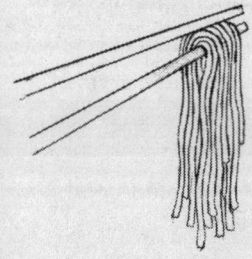

Duncan was wolfing his down ecstatically. Kara, on the other hand, carefully speared a toasted, cream-colored grub, delicately put it in her mouth and slowly chewed.

"Huh," she said, "It's pretty good. Kinda sweet and chewy in my mouth." She followed it with a whole forkful of noodles.

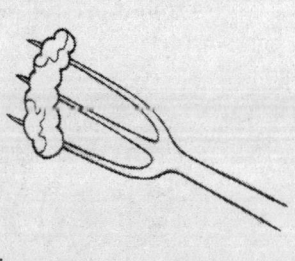

"You know, there are those who like to eat them while they're still alive!" Alex decided to throw in.

Kara and Duncan both swallowed, looked at each other and grimaced, "Ewwww!"

"I know!" agreed Alex, and they all made faces but continued eating with gusto.

"Do you like the sauce?" Alex asked, obviously very pleased with herself. "I trained as a saucier when

I was younger. They told me I had tasty hands."

Kara, mid chew, nodded enthusiastically.

"Mmmmm! Very saucy!" Duncan chimed in.

"So, Kara," Alex steered the conversation, "tell us about this spell of yours."

"Oh!" Kara rummaged in her bag and found the large spell book. "My Gran gave me this, it's really, really old. I already have the vaporizing agent, and the personal items..." Kara pulled out a small stone bowl with a lid tied on, and rattled the contents.

"And now I need a piece of this blue coral." She tipped the book so Duncan and Alex could see the picture.

"Ooo! Pretty!" said Duncan.

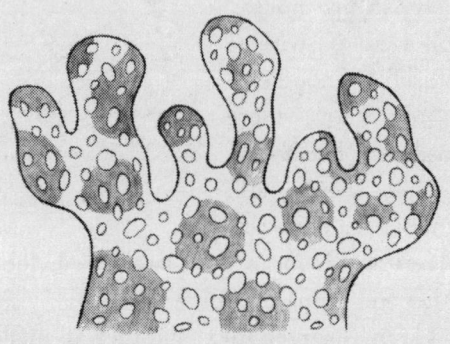

"And it's not actually coral, it's this algae called coraline that looks like coral." She paused, her finger running along the page, "It says the only known location is Logue's Butte."

Duncan and Alex looked at each other.

"It must be near the ocean, but I couldn't find it on my map," Kara continued, puzzled.

"Uh, we know where that is, but it's a long way from the ocean," Duncan offered, equally perplexed.

"The Logue family were friends of ours," Alex said, "but they were run off long before you were born. It's called Poulot's Plateau now, about twenty miles west of here."

"Ohhh." She looked back at her book. "And lastly I need some powdered cyclops horn." She looked up at Duncan, suddenly embarrassed.

"Cyclops horn, eh?" Alex said with a grin. "Well, we can certainly help you with that." She retrieved her spice grater from the kitchen. "How much d' ya need?"

Kara looked down at the book, "It says a pinch."

Alex lifted the grater and Duncan cringed away slightly.

"Oh, come on ya big baby." She grabbed his horn and straightened out his head, smirking, "It's just like when you bite your nails."

Duncan slowly pulled all his hands under the table. "I don't bite my nails," he quietly protested.

"Okay, hold the bowl up," Alex instructed.

Three quick gentle strokes and it was done.

"Good?" she asked.

"Good!" Kara replied.

Duncan tentatively touched the tip of his horn.

"Now the coral..." Alex considered with some trepidation, "that might be more difficult."

Kara looked very worried.

"But we'll cross that bridge when we come to it! For right now, we need to figure out everything we need for the trip."

"We?" Kara said, taken by surprise.

"Of course we're coming with you," Alex stated matter-of-factly. "This is a classic three person job. Very dangerous."

"Definitely three people," agreed Duncan, "and we'll all need disguises! We can't just go waltzing in there. We'd be about as popular as a flame in a flourmill."

Kara was all kinds of confused.

"Oh yeah, there'd be some fireworks," Duncan went on, "and running and screaming and pushing and shoving and tripping and falling..."

Alex shook her head as he spun off into his own little world of words. She gave Kara a reassuring look and a pat on the shoulder. They spent the next several hours planning, gathering and packing before finally getting some sleep.

Dinner

"There's no need to apologize and don't concern yourself with impropriety. I will personally see to it that the appropriate precautionary measures are taken, though I'm sure there's nothing to worry about and the situation will soon resolve itself." Minister James spoke in a distracted monotone to the image of Kara's mother but, before she could thank him, he waved his hand and the crystal ball cleared.

"That sound is disgusting. He's had enough."

Dragon, eyes closed, snout submerged in brownish gray gruel, was quietly lapping from a shallow bowl. At the Minister's command, the servant lowered the bowl, but Dragon continued to flick his tongue in and out, spattering goo.

"Stop! Stop!" whispered the distressed

servant as he frantically tried to clean up.

The Minister glared. "Leave," he said icily.

The servant froze, then hurriedly exited.

Once he was alone, the Minister approached a full-length mirror and studied himself, turning his face slightly to the left, then right. On a shelf to one side, he reached toward several glass jars containing various body parts from various creatures and selected two six-inch spiral horns. He held them against his forehead and they instantly attached to his skull. He dropped his hands and again turned from side to side, then removed the horns, bored with his whimsy.

He continued to stare at the mirror, running his fingertips along his receding hairline. Moving closer, he inspected the line of his once broken nose and pulled at a wrinkle at the corner of his eye. Closer still, he examined the symmetry of his eyebrows, then plucked out a single hair which he put delicately in his mouth and, almost imperceptibly, chewed.

Still dissatisfied, he reached up toward an intricate brass contraption that was attached to the wall. It unfolded in front of the mirror with a series of lenses lining up one in front of the next. The Minister's hair may once have been blond, but his manicured mustache was dark and resembled a line of tall thin trees as he gazed at it through the

Dinner

magnifying apparatus.

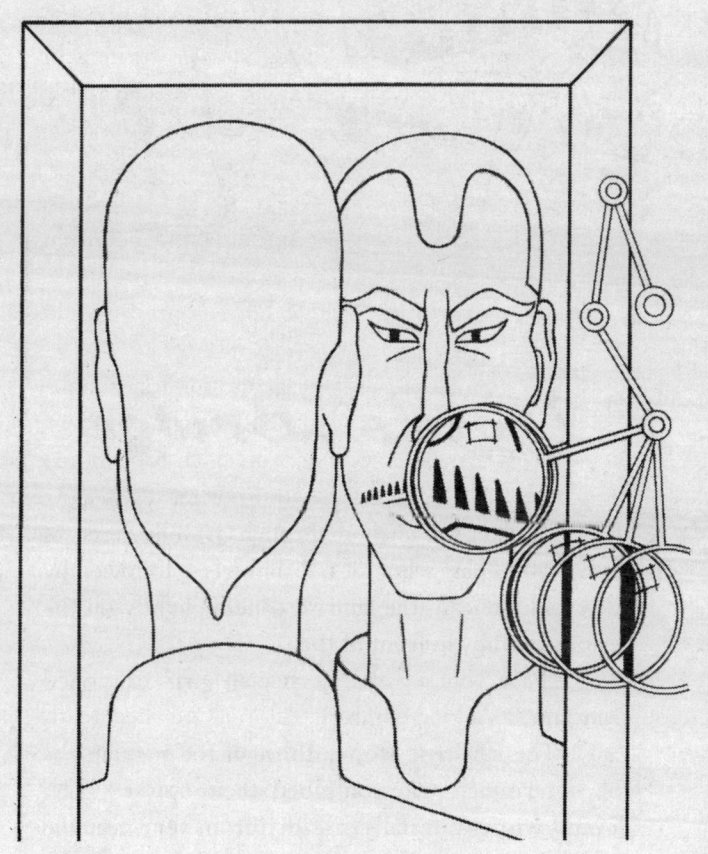

Logues' Bridge

Footsteps crunched through gravelly scree as Kara trotted past a line of tall thin trees, followed by Alex and Duncan, the sunrise dancing lightly on the serious journey in front of them.

"Pace yourself there, cheetah girl," cautioned Duncan. "It's a long climb."

The sun rose slowly through the morning as the determined trio continued their upward hike. Several wispy waterfalls cascaded from very near the top of the majestic butte looming ever larger in the distance.

Logues' Bridge

"I thought it was closer," said Kara. "It feels like we'll never get there."

"Ah, then perhaps a change of perspective would help," offered Duncan. With a big grin, he scooped her up and set her on his broad shoulder. She smiled back gratefully and stretched out her aching legs.

Many more miles were behind them when Alex, rounding a massive tangle of brambles, perked up and pointed at an old wooden sign.

"There it is," she announced as they approached a deep narrow canyon at the base of the massive cliff.

"Logue's Butte," she and Kara read aloud though the carved lettering was worn and barely discernable.

Duncan had stopped and was staring at an old weathered suspension bridge.

"Oooh boy," he exhaled.

"It doesn't look too bad," Kara said, noticing his hesitation. She hopped down and stepped toward the cliff edge then carefully peered into the deep crevasse. "Oooh. That's a long way down."

"Was it always that far?" Duncan wondered.

"It still looks pretty strong though, you know, structural?" said Alex, striding cavalierly out onto the rough gray boards.

"No wait! Wait!" cried Duncan, engulfed by visions of Alex plummeting to her death.

She stopped and turned then walked back off.

"Oh babe, I think you're remembering it being a lot scarier than it really was. You were just a kid the last time. That was so long ago."

"And that makes it even worse! It's been rained on for fifty years since then. They don't call water the universal solvent for nothing."

"Universal solvent?" Kara asked quizzically.

"No, no. He's right," Alex countered. "So what are we gonna do?"

Duncan squatted down beside the bench and said, "Okay Woody, I've got a dangerous mission for you."

"Woody?" Kara and Alex asked in unison.

"Buddy was just a nickname," he replied, then

cooed, "Wasn't it, Woody, wasn't it?"

Kara and Alex shrugged at each other as Duncan placed a hand on the bench and said very seriously, "I need you on point." It didn't move. He sighed worriedly. "Carefully, now, go to the far side and stay there." This time, it lifted and floated across, the boards reacting slightly to its proximity with creaking ropes and falling dust.

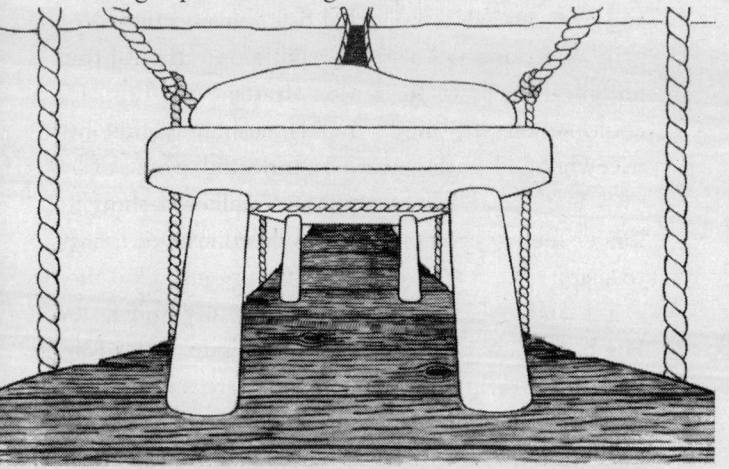

"Well, big guy, I think there's only one thing to do," Alex said decidedly. "You're gonna have to go first and make sure it's safe. If it'll hold you, it'll hold us."

Duncan nodded and nervously patted himself down, "Hammer, machete, tent…ok, I'm ready." He breathed out heavily.

"You can do it, babe. You always said it was the 'most loftiest' thing you ever did." Her voice seemed to fade as he started onto the wobbly planks.

"More like the most stupidest thing I ever did," he said, mostly to himself.

His progress was scary and slow. Perspiring profusely, biting his lip, cursing under his breath, he felt the bridge creaking with every careful step. Over and over, his white knuckled fists released their iron grip and, one at a time, slid along the fibrous umbilical cords to their next strategic position. He could smell the angry rapids rushing far below, overwhelmed as they were by the acrid aroma of his own fear sweat. He cringed, eye squeezed shut, no longer feeling his feet, positive the ropes were about to snap.

Suddenly, the creaking got louder and faster. His heart was racing, about to explode when Kara jumped onto his back, piggy style, arms around his neck. He forced his eye open to see the ground solid beneath him. Alex gave him a cute little swat on the behind as she, too, stepped off the bridge.

"My hero!" Kara said, pulling herself up to give him a kiss on the cheek before jumping back down.

Alex walked around, stretched up as tall as she could and kissed his other cheek, "You're my hero, too."

Logues' Bridge

Duncan's eye darted behind him, "Yeah, that wasn't...too bad." He inhaled a reprieve and walked the few steps to the base of the two thousand foot high basalt butte.

"Oooh. That's a long way up," said Kara.

"Ha! Simple as Soup!" bragged Duncan, full of bravado, the bridge completely forgotten. "Climbing is what Quadrapuses do best. It's just a matter of focus." He gestured toward the rock wall using two hands on each side of his head like horse blinders.

"But first I think we should focus on some of my famous ergot-free ashen rye griddlecakes," tempted Alex, taking off her backpack. "Even heroes need to eat."

"Mmmm, griddlecakes!" Kara and Duncan said together as they bounded over.

"With blackberry sauce flambé!" added Alex with a flourish, her eyes growing huge as she looked past her hungry companions.

Sambuka Black

A shadow fell over the two and they spun to see an enormous, dark blue, knuckle-walking, quasi-simian, horned lizard monster clenching a long bone between its way-too-many sharp teeth.

Kara gasped, paralyzed with fear, as Duncan stepped gingerly towards it.

"Hey boy! Hey boy! Who's a good boy? Gimme the bone! C'mon, gimme the bone!" The spiky beast dropped its prize, dropped to its elbows with its butt in the air, and wagged its spiny, plated tail as it panted around its lolling forked tongue, silvery threads of drool dripping down. Duncan picked up the damp plaything and threw it across the canyon. The creature easily leapt the gap and scampered after it.

"Dinorillas! I love those guys!" he declared with a wide grin, then back to the girls, "Who's starving?"

"Whaaa…" was all that escaped Kara's way-too-dry-throat.

"Oh no," said Alex, rummaging in their packs, "I forgot tinder for the fire piston." She perused the area's slight offerings, most plants still quite green for so late in the year. "But I'm sure there's something dry around here somewhere."

"I have a fire stone!" Kara announced, finding her voice again. "What's a fire piston?"

"It's a tube inside a tube that makes a hot coal," Duncan answered animatedly. "What's a fire stone?"

"Oh. Oh, it's this rock my dad gave me, he calls it White Bright. You shave some off into a little pile then, when you strike a spark into it, it'll flare up. It's just like tinder, but also works when it's wet. You need a knife, though, 'cuz it needs to be small like dust." She whittled a tiny amount onto the ground.

"Ooo, pretty," said Duncan as he took out the fire piston and knelt down beside her.

Holding the small device so Kara could see, he showed how the hardwood tube was solid at one end, then pulled out the inner rod and showed how its concave tip was filled with a pea-sized ball of fluff. He smeared a dollop of cooking fat around the outside of the tip, which was wrapped with a few turns of thread to make an airtight seal, and reinserted the rod, forcing it almost all the way in.

"Okay, this is the tricky part," he said as he raised a hand over the end of the plunger then quickly and precisely slammed the two pieces all the way together. With a satisfied smile, he pulled the rod out and tapped a slightly-smaller-than-pea-sized coal onto the pile of White Bright. Kara clapped her approval as it flashed into a bright white flame.

A half hour later, the full-tummied trio sat at the edge of the craggy ledge, feet dangling, appreciating the view.

"...he could have found that anywhere. Those claws are for ripping apart old logs. They live on mushrooms and bark and stuff like that."

The giant bony head nudged him again and dropped its toy. Duncan tossed it in a long high arc as the dinorilla gave chase once more.

He began to chuckle, "Heh heh heh. Remember that time at the beach..." Alex began to chuckle, too, and finished the sentence with him, "when all the raccoons came running out!" They both threw their heads back and howled riotously, Duncan reaching up to wipe away a tear.

Kara looked back and forth between the two expecting more details, but none were forthcoming.

When their laughter finally died down, Alex sighed, "Ahhh. Now this is nice."

"Yeah, but, that cliff isn't going to climb itself." Duncan sprang up then squatted down behind Alex, planting kisses on the back of her neck.

"Stop, stop, Kara doesn't want to see that," she blushed.

"I just wanted to thank you for lunch," he nuzzled.

"It's okay. My mom and dad do that all the time, I'm used to it. Sorta," said Kara, pretending to inspect her fingernails.

Duncan stepped back over and lifted Kara to her feet, "Ali-oop! What's say we pack up and let the cook rest a bit longer?"

"Okay!" Kara agreed.

They buried the cooking coals under a nice thick layer of dirt, stuffed the pan, plates and jars away in their bundles and tied all the gear back onto the bench, with Duncan pausing every minute or so to throw the bone one last time.

Logue's Butte

Kara and Alex skipped slowly and gently along the rocky surface as they followed Duncan, his heavy calloused feet slapping hard one ahead of the other. The pleats of his kilt fanning out beneath him, he ascended vertically as easily as if he were crawling across the ground, climbing hand over hand over hand over hand grasping at any crack, crag or ledge.

The girls sat comfortably on either end of the bench, which dangled on a rope from Duncan's waist, occasionally kicking at the cliff wall to keep from banging into it. Below, the dinorilla sat on its haunches whining pitifully.

Kara leaned out and called down apologetically, "Sorry boy, we gotta go," then,

"Whoa!" as she started to lose her balance. Alex's quick and steadying hand helped ease Kara's pounding heart from her throat and back into her chest where it belonged.

"Best not to look down," Alex wisely advised, as Kara nodded her emphatic agreement and lifted her gaze skyward. "Oh good lord, don't look up either, best to just look straight ahead. I do like being up high, though," she reflected, changing the subject. "Kyle used to fly us all over the place, you could see everything!"

"Really?!"

"Yeah, there's nothing as profound as riding a dragon," she continued with a faraway sparkle in her eyes. "I mean, just to feel his massive shoulder muscles flex between his wings. Kyle would soar soooo high and then nosedive into clouds as fast as he could…they actually go *poof!*"

"But weren't you frightened?"

"Scared white! But it was exhilarating! Duncan's arms around me made me feel safe and Kyle was amazing…he loved showing off for the lady dragons! His agility was better than dragons half his size and he could out fly all of them."

"But I thought only the Minister was allowed to fly."

"Well, now," said Alex bitterly.

"Rock!" yelled Duncan from above.

Logue's Butte

"Ouch!" yelped Alex as a tiny stone bounced off her skull.

"Sorry..."

"It's okay, babe, I'm alright." She gingerly touched her forehead, "Oof, that left a bump."

"You're gonna have a horn like Duncan," Kara teased. They giggled and swung as he continued to grunt and strain above them.

The sun had reached its zenith and its warmth was in full effect when the first hand appeared at the edge of the cliff, followed by a second and a third then Duncan's glistening face and torso. Panting like the dinorilla, he reached back with his fourth hand and pulled the rope high over his head raising the bench to his waist so Kara and Alex could safely disembark.

They climbed over his shoulders and tried to help him up, if only symbolically. Wild eyed and drenched in sweat, Duncan barely made it over the edge before flopping on his back, gulping air like it was water. "I…hate…climbing…" he squeaked out between breaths.

While Kara ran ahead, Alex squatted down and lovingly patted his heaving chest, "You take all the time you need there, Mr. Soup." She smiled and handed him the drinking gourd. He sat up, gulping water like it was air.

"Rainbow Crackers! Blue Bubbles! It's beautiful!"

"Yes it is," agreed Alex as she joined Kara. "The wasps don't like it up this high…but the bees do," she added, nervously glancing about.

They waded into a sea of multicolored flowers that covered nearly the entire plateau.

"It used to be like this everywhere in the old days," Alex continued wistfully.

Logue's Butte

"Everywhere?! What happened?"

"The grubs, beetles and wasps aren't eaten by the dragons anymore, so they overpopulate. And then they eat everything in sight. Flowers are their favorite."

"I knew dragons could live on bugs!" Kara declared. Then she noticed a distant structure made of huge blocks of stone, "And what's that?!"

"Not even the dragons know. Knew. It's been here forever. Some kind of cathedral I guess." Alex started towards it gesturing for Kara to follow.

Off to either side, they could see stone ramps overgrown with lush vegetation.

"Hey, those look like the teeter totters my dad builds," Kara said as a refreshed Duncan caught up and scampered past, trailed by the bench. He ran up to the thirty-foot tall center stone, stopped, bent down and picked up one of the small white pebbles that surrounded the cathedral.

As Kara wondered how they were going to get inside, Duncan turned sharply right and walked directly into the crack between the blocks. She blinked as he disappeared before her eyes.

Alex saw Kara's reaction and laughed as she trotted ahead. "C'mon! You're gonna love it on the inside," and she, too, disappeared.

Kara approached and realized the giant blocks formed a circle, open to the sky, and what looked like the front stone was actually a gap that revealed the ring's interior stone surface. She also saw that Duncan was squatted down off to the right, studying something. "What a funny illusion, hiding a doorway in plain sight," she mused.

Even more surprising, the area inside was substantially smaller than expected and the blocks were now only waist high, the surrounding field of flowers clearly visible.

"Pretty magical huh?" asked Alex, off to the left.

Logue's Butte

"My dad would say it's all in the math," replied Kara, fascinated. Looking around then down at the ground, she examined a flat, ten-foot diameter slab with simple patterns carved into it. "Hey, this all looks like granite, how'd it get up here?" She then joined Alex studying similar designs carved into the walls.

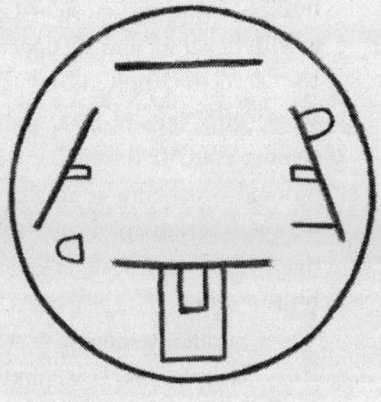

"Kyle brought us up here when we were kids," Alex reminisced, then whispered, "Duncan used chalk to draw boobies on the pictographs!" Kara giggled.

Alex turned to see Duncan with the white rock in his hand, apparently adding something rude to one of the designs. Eyebrows raised, she waved furiously at him behind Kara's back. Guiltily, he used two of his hands to erase whatever he'd been drawing. Kara, however, was preoccupied with the carvings and didn't notice.

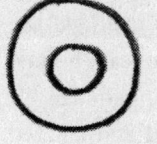

Alex looked around, but a little aimlessly, "I don't see any coral.

I wonder if the book was talking about some kind of flower? But, it's supposed to be underwater, ri-?"

"Hey, this rock feels soft," said Duncan as he walked across the circular center stone. Alex scuffed it with her hoof and shrugged.

"Yeah, a hundred feet underwater," Kara answered, "but it is a very old book, maybe it's wrong. Wait. It looks like this carving!" She reached out and touched a coral shaped design, then turned and again fixed upon the designs on the central slab.

Suddenly she got very excited.

"Hey! This is a picture of those things out there!" She started to climb over the wall.

"NO!!!" roared Duncan. He lunged and grabbed her arm just as she threw her leg over the other side. Kara inhaled sharply and froze, confronted by the thirty-foot drop.

"Whoa! I forgot." Heart thumping and breathless, she let Duncan set her back down on solid ground. They walked out through the gap and Kara ran over to one of the granite seesaws.

"The drawings say we have to move this." She cleared some of the brush and tried to dislodge the large rock sitting on the low end. Duncan helped push and it slid off the ramp. Nothing happened.

Kara climbed up to the high end and started

jumping up and down. Slowly it tipped, allowing an attached, rusted chain to disappear into a small hole in the ground.

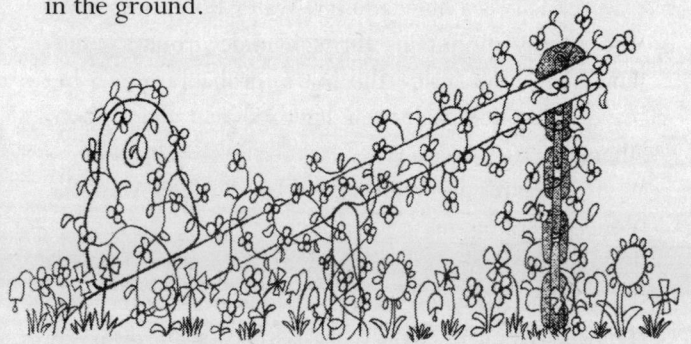

The roar of the nearby waterfall began to quiet and she ran to the cliff edge in time to see the stream slow to a trickle. She furrowed her brow, thinking, then her eyes widened.

"Yes!!" She jumped up and ran back. "I think I know what's happening! C'mon, we have to do the others!" They went to each of the three remaining ramps and repeated the process.

"Now back to the cathedral!" she proclaimed.

Inside the structure, she held her arms out to keep Duncan and Alex off the stone disk. They heard a low scraping rumble and slowly, very slowly, a granite cylinder began to rise out of the ground.

Duncan was astonished, "Holy crow, that's some big magic!"

"It's not magic, it's buoyancy!" Kara said,

gleefully playing the scholar. Her students shrugged, a little lost.

"This is a huge aquifer! Water flows here from the nearby mountains through underground cracks and pushes up inside the butte, probably into a big cave. I bet it's at least a hundred feet deep down there!"

"So, it's an underground lake?" asked Alex, the concept sinking in.

"Yep!"

The rounded piece of rock was taller than Duncan when it came to rest, revealing a doorway into its hollow interior. "And I think this is like an elevator!" added Kara, the sound of rushing water growing to a roar once again.

"What's that soun…"

"It's okay," reassured Kara, "It's just spillways like in our fish trap back home." She rushed over to the doorway and peered inside, but it was too dark to see anything.

Alex looked inside too and said, "I'll go wake up some of our glowy friends," before trotting away. Duncan and Kara knelt down and continued to peer into the blackness.

"What now?"

Kara was still puzzling, "Well, I haven't quite figured that part out yet, but there's definitely water down there."

"Yeah, I can smell it."

"The coral's probably growing on the bottom."

"How do you have all this in your head? Is that magic?" Duncan asked admiringly.

"No, I just read a lot."

"Oh yeah! Me too! Well, I read the pictures anyway."

"Duncan, can I ask you a question?"

"Sure ya can."

She bit her lip, "Do you miss your arms?"

"Well, it's been such a long time, I'm kinda used to it now. But sometimes I think I can still feel them, trying to help out."

Just then, Alex returned with fireflies in the empty flour jar.

"Glow bugs!" Kara exclaimed.

She held the jar inside the granite tube and they could see a floor and another doorway about fifteen feet below.

"Okay. I think, if we go through that door, we'll get to the water," Kara reasoned.

"I'll go! I love the water!" Duncan volunteered. He stretched across the tube, braced himself with his hands and feet, and started climbing down.

"Wait! It'll be really deep!"

"That's okay. I can hold my breath for a long, long time." He started down again.

"Wait! I have an idea." Kara waved him back up. She pulled the map from her pocket and poured it out onto the ground, held the empty bottle near his head and *thoomp!* it slipped from her hands and swallowed his horn and forehead stopping just short of his eyebrow.

He looked up toward his distorted skull, apparently not in any pain, "Uhhh…"

She pulled it off and tried again, this time successfully. Duncan's seemingly tiny head was completely enclosed in the bottle.

"There! Now you'll have lots of air. You know, for breathing!"

He smiled and said in a high echoing voice, "Brilliant!"

Alex held up her jar of glow bugs. "And light, you know, for seeing!"

They all smiled then Kara said, "I bet we could get lots more glow bugs in there!"

"I bet you're right!" Alex agreed. "Ladies and gentlemen…?" she called lightly and a cloud of fireflies gathered around them. Kara held the jar this time and the whole swarm filed in comfortably, the glow growing brighter and brighter until it was almost blinding. She handed it to Duncan.

"Really brilliant!" and like a giant spider, he descended into the tube and through the lower door.

The Depths

He had to hunch over to follow the narrow tunnel as it curved and dropped gently and, after only a few seconds, he came to the other end to find water lapping at his feet.

Duncan held up the light inside a rough walled chamber and saw the granite tube disappear into the rock ceiling above and into the water below. After delicately testing with one toe, he grimaced, sighed deeply, then bravely jumped in.

It was even colder than he expected and he kicked furiously and paddled with three arms hoping this part of the adventure would be short. His upper right hand held out the light, but all he could see was the side of the cylinder vanishing into the gloom. He followed it down for several yards before reaching the end then noticed that its underside looked weird, almost reflective like a black wavy mirror.

He flipped around and slowly pushed the light, then his tiny bottled head, up into the tube, breaking the surface while treading water. He gazed around inside the cavernous air bubble, the sides of the tube impossibly far away, but then started to shiver and dropped back down into the dark abyss.

Swimming deeper and deeper, his ears began to hurt and the sound of his own breathing began to fade. He squeezed his eye shut, wiggled his jaw and *pop!* sound rushed back into his head. He opened his eye to see a small eel snaking past his face, its lateral stripes luminous and flashing. A moment later, he passed a school of tiny translucent fish, his skin reflecting starkly white in their glow.

He began to wonder if he was still moving downward when the vague outline of a giant cylinder appeared and suddenly the floor of the aquifer was rushing up at him. He swept his arms forward and reverse paddled, causing fine silty debris to swirl up and obscure his view. Gently kicking away from the engulfing clouds, he examined the area within his small sphere of illumination.

The blue coral was everywhere and every inch in between was filled with wiggling tubes, pulsing blobs, glowing colored spots, things swimming around eating things and other things swimming around getting eaten. Trying not to disturb any of the small residents, Duncan reached out and broke off a

The Depths

chunk of coral and put it in a pocket. A writhing white worm twitched by and he lifted his head to stare right into an eye the size of a wagon wheel. It took a moment to register before his mouth opened and the bottle vibrated with a tiny high-pitched scream. Tentacles, teeth and claws overwhelmed his imagination as a spasming flurry of arms and legs rocketed him back toward the surface.

He was so spooked, he launched from the water, sprinted through the tunnel, scrambled up the tube and out the doorway, then flattened himself against the outside of the cylinder, heart racing, panting heavily, and in his squeaky bottled voice said, "I hate the water..."

He retrieved the coral from his pocket and handed it to a worshipful Kara. She waved him down and removed the bottle.

"Are you okay? Was it scary down there?"

"Nah, just really cold," came Duncan's usual voice from his regular sized head. He began squeezing water from the bottom of his saturated kilt. "But I think whoever built all this may be related to you."

"Related? To me?"

"Uh huh, and your dad and your grandmother. The tube elevator thing? It's waaay bigger on the inside."

"Wow. Now that's an interesting theory," Alex agreed as she released the glow bugs, thanking them for their help with a dollop of blackberry sauce.

Kara speculated giddily about the idea of ancient engineering ancestors as she and Duncan reversed the seesaws.

"I wonder how they made it. Where did the granite come from? How did they tunnel out the spillways? How did they know how big to make them?" She paused for a moment, "But it's funny, I have a book all about modern inventions that use the power of water and it doesn't mention anything like this. I mean, it couldn't have been my ancestors. How would people forget that they could do this kind of thing?"

"Well, it didn't take long for people to forget dragons could talk," Duncan noted.

"Oooo, good point. My mom calls that 'touché'."

"Tushy? Like derrière?"

"Haha! No! Too-shay, it means 'good point'."

Once the lower spillways were open and Duncan had discovered every possible way of pronouncing touché, they joined Alex back inside the cathedral as she finished repacking their gear. Together they watched the secret elevator seat itself back into the ground.

"Good as new," said Duncan a he bounced up and down on the top, feeling the slight undulation of the floating granite tube.

"Leave nothing but your footprints," quoted Alex.

Duncan picked up the bench and tucked it under his lower right arm as they all strolled through the fragrant flowers toward the edge of the plateau. Kara was distracted by the breathtaking panoramic view and a little sad to be leaving. She glanced back in the direction of her village while Alex climbed up onto Duncan's right shoulder.

"I wish there was an easier way back down," said Kara.

"Oh, there is," Duncan replied.

"Duncan, wait! You can't just…" Alex tried to stop him, but he scooped Kara up, plopped her on his left shoulder, pulled the tarp from his belt and started to sprint.

"Hang on tight!" he yelled.

"AaaaaaaaAAAAAAH!" Kara replied and wrapped her arms around his head.

Duncan leapt from the cliff and whipped out the stretchy cloth, gripping leather loops at each of the four corners, and it inflated like a sheet blowing on a clothesline. He positioned the bench between his knees, ankles crossed, then took one of the two loops from his upper right hand and used all four arms to manipulate the tarp. He managed to slow their out-of-control spiraling descent and gracefully guided them away from the butte.

Kara forced one eye open. "Oh! That's a long way down!"

"Yeah, but look at all this room! Nothing to bang your horn on," honked Duncan with a nasally twang.

Kara's legs were wrapped around Duncan's upper arm, ankles crossed, her right arm around his neck, her left hand gripping his nose.

"Sorry!" she sputtered, grabbing his horn instead.

"That's alright," Duncan replied wiggling his face around. "I did kinda surprise you with that whole leaping-off-the-cliff thing."

"Look, over there," said Alex, pointing to the horizon. "It's the city."

They could see the skyline of the industrial port city, angular and geometric, set between the craggy coastal mountains, the ocean glistening beyond.

"We should be there in two days."

"Get ready to jump," Duncan announced.

"More jumping?!" Kara cried.

"I haven't really perfected my landings yet," he admitted sheepishly.

"It's easy," Alex reassured her, "just watch me."

As they neared the treetops, Duncan pulled down on the back two corners of the tarp causing their decent to slow for a moment. Alex, then Kara, gently and quite easily stepped off Duncan's shoulders and grabbed the tops of soft conifers. They began sliding and climbing down while cringing to the sounds of crashing and cursing and breaking

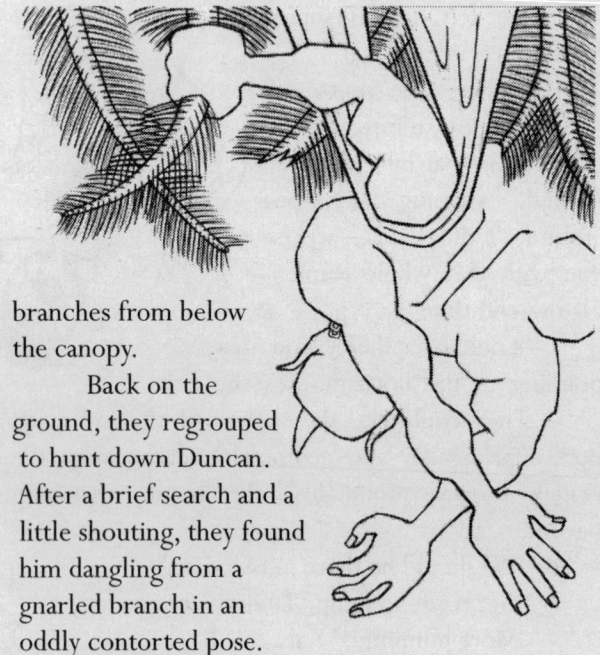

branches from below the canopy.

Back on the ground, they regrouped to hunt down Duncan. After a brief search and a little shouting, they found him dangling from a gnarled branch in an oddly contorted pose.

"I'm okay! Where's Mr. Woods? I dropped him, is he alright?"

"Mr. Woods?" Kara asked.

"The bench…you know, after braving the bridge and all, I thought…"

While Duncan untangled himself, the girls poked around and found the bench nearby, floating serenely upside down but undamaged. Duncan, however, was not. Alex pointed to his obviously dislocated shoulder, his arm twisted horribly behind

The Depths

his back, and like a dog chasing its tail, he turned in circles trying to find it.

Finally he stopped, sighed, and looked at the ground, then quietly, "A little noise."

Alex looked away and plugged her ears and nodded knowingly at Kara to do the same. Even so, they heard a sickening *CRUNCH!* followed by a shriek, then Duncan trotted by like nothing had happened, asking, "Who wants fish?"

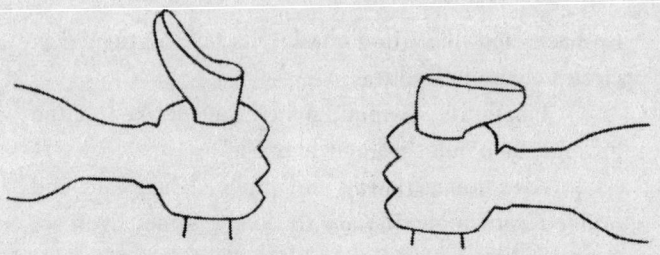

Fishing & Camping

Lying on his stomach, Duncan looked over the riverbank. "There's three nice big ones right below us."

Kara, beside him, leaned on a fallen tree and squinted at the bright surface reflections. "How can you see?" she asked.

"Can't. I can hear 'em."

"Fish talk?"

"Well, it's really more of a constant annoying whining," he said with a contemptuous squint, then brightly, "Here, try my scoop."

As Kara examined the telescoping net, Duncan grabbed her by the ankles and flipped her

Fishing & Camping

upside down over the rushing water. She squealed, then giggled furiously as she plunged the net in.

"Whoa, be careful there!" cried Alex.

"She's fine," Duncan called back, "light as a feather!"

Just then a big yellow bee buzzed past his nose.

"Oh no..." said Alex.

"I got one!!" Kara exclaimed.

Duncan dropped her and ran.

Kara's leg scraped against the fallen tree and her bootlace hooked on a broken branch.

"DUNCAN!" screamed Alex, sprinting to the river to find Kara dangling and thrashing, her head and shoulders underwater. She wrapped her arms around Kara's free leg and managed to drag her to safety while Kara coughed and choked and refused to drop the netted fish.

Rubbing a little bit too roughly, Alex used the bottom of her shirt to try to dry Kara's hair, then forced a smile and set off after Duncan.

They eventually tracked him down at the base of a huge oak tree. Duncan was covered head to toe by an angry swarm of bees, stinging mercilessly as he stood there, dazed and oblivious, licking honey from his fingers.

"Can't you tell them to stop?!" Kara implored.

"They wouldn't listen. They have important work to do. He gets what he deserves," Alex replied coldly.

Kara was bewildered and obviously upset and finally, after a long silence, Alex yelled, "DUNCAN! SHE COULD HAVE DROWNED!"

Duncan came out of his stupor and realized he was in a lot of pain. He staggered around drunkenly, swatting clumsily at his attackers.

Alex, quieter but still very angry, "And you know they die when they sting you!" She turned and stormed away.

Alex, Kara and the bench climbed a slight rise, silhouetted against the aurora borealis dancing across the darkening sky.

Duncan, covered in welts, followed a short distance behind, head down, shoulders sagging and still a little off balance. Occasional bees pursued him and he flinched, trying to gently wave them away.

At the crest of the hill, Alex stopped and looked around. "This'll make a good camp." She turned, walked straight to Duncan without making eye contact and quickly hugged him sideways, ending the conflict. "I think it's time to cook up that fine fat

Fishing & Camping

fish of yours," she said brightly as she walked back toward Kara.

"It's all in the preparation, right?" said Kara timidly, still a little uncomfortable.

"Actually, these guys are so good," she winked, then, gesturing over her shoulder, "even ol' Duncan there could fix 'em like a gourmet."

As Alex went about the messy business of cleaning the fish, Kara gathered some wood and cleared a spot for a fire. This time, however, after shaving the White Bright, she held out a piece of flint and struck it sharply with her knife. A spark flew into the pile and *poof!* She had a small flame to which she fed twigs, then sticks until it grew into a fine cooking size.

Meanwhile, Duncan, humming obsessively to himself, whizzed around as he stripped the branches from a sapling, pounded in four stakes, then whipped out the tarp like a big tablecloth. It floated down over the sapling and he secured the four corners to the stakes, resulting in a tight, pyramid shaped tent.

Kara watched him over her shoulder, "Wow. He's all over the place."

Alex was genuinely amused, "Yes, he certainly is that."

When he was finished, he sat down on a log next to the girls, crossed his arms, and rocked back and forth, "Ya know how your brain gets stuck in a song and ya sing it over and over and over and it just won't go away no matter how many times you wash your head out with soap? Well, it's like that but it's a haiku. And it's in my knee." Duncan pulled his knee up to his ear, a spooked expression on his face.

"Honey hangover," Alex explained, "He'll be okay."

Relieved that she had brought a change of clothes, Kara laid her damp ones by the fire, then sat down and pulled out her little bowl so she could complete her spell recipe. She broke up a piece of the coral and, using the curving handle of the upside down lid, ground it into the horn and shell mixture. Though blue on the outside, the coral broke down into brightly colored swirls as it was crushed and stirred. After staring at the sparkly mixture for a while, she dropped the Minister's gold button back in, tied the lid back on and put it away.

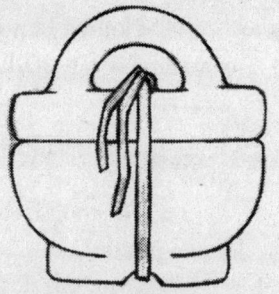

Duncan was staring into the campfire as Alex sprinkled spices on the cooking fish. He licked his lips and rested his chin in his upper hands, "She's using her magic powder!"

Kara started at the mention of magic. "Magic? What does it do?"

"It makes it taste better!" He said, fluttering all of his fingers, yet completely serious.

"It's basil," Alex confided.

Fully fed, Duncan entertained by creating shadows on the side of the tent.

"I know, I know," cheered Kara. "It's a dragon, watching a cat, stalking a bunny rabbit, who's eating a carrot!"

"Yes!" clapped Duncan proudly. "Now you do one!"

"Oh, no, I couldn't do...wait, I could show you a puzzle?"

"Ooo, puzzles. I'm good at those."

Kara pulled out her sketchbook and, with a piece of charcoal, drew a series of arrows. "Ok, this is a simple code for an ordinary word. What is it?"

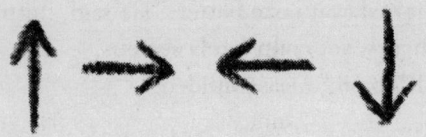

Duncan twisted his head this way and that, studying the markings.

"I give up," he finally said.

"NEWS!" said Kara. "See? North, East, West, South."

"Ahhh," nodded Duncan wisely. "I don't get it."

"Don't worry babe," cooed Alex. "Some people are puzzle smart, some people are carrying smart."

"Yeah! And darn proud of it. I come from a long line of carriers. Ya know," his nostrils flared, "we should get under cover, it smells like rain."

Duncan stretched up the edge of the tarp for the bench and the girls then crawled inside himself. The three adventurers settled down for the night as fading firelight flickered across their tired faces and a light shower started pattering on the tent.

"Sounds like we got inside just in time," observed Duncan as he curled up behind Alex and wrapped three of his arms around her, his fourth tucked back under his head.

Kara fluffed up her bag to use as a pillow and pulled her cape around her like a blanket. With eyes half closed, she looked toward her companions and said, "Thanks for helping me."

"We never pass up a good mission," replied a gallant Alex, and Duncan grinned his solidarity.

Knowing that nothing could stop them, Kara drifted off to sleep.

"When it gets dark, I'll sneak around and do some sculpulating," said Duncan.

"Some what?"

"Sculpulating. Ya know, look around."

"Scrutinizing?" offered Alex as she negotiated the steep mountain path.

"No, no! You know…" he stomped along behind her, "Check the lay of the land. Plan escape routes."

"You mean...reconnoitering."

"No, that's not it. I'm sure it's sculpul...wait. Did I make that up? I mean, it's a good word and bears repeat-"

Alex whacked him on the hip and pointed, "Look! There!"

They stopped and stared at a pure white billy goat, bathed in beautiful beams of sunlight in a small clearing next to the path. It calmly chewed on some thorny blackberry vines.

"A goat!" she exclaimed excitedly.

"I'll be damned. They *are* real," said Duncan quietly, awestruck. Alex nodded knowingly.

Fishing & Camping

"Hey you guys! What're all these holes?" Kara called from farther down the trail.

"Holes?" Alex caught up with Kara who was poking a stick at little dark pockets in the ground.

Her eyes got huge, "RUN!!!"

She grabbed Kara's wrist and pulled her along but they were instantly pursued by a pair of grotesque hawk sized wasps. Kara saw that they were the same as the one from her garden but much, much bigger.

Alex shrugged out of her backpack and swung it wildly, screaming for Duncan. He came charging up and pulled Kara behind him, flailing at the speeding insects with his hands and machete.

Kara, back to back with him, grabbed the telescoping net from his waistband and whipped her head around trying to follow the angry buzzing. She swung desperately and snagged one of the bugs, but it was so big and fast it nearly pulled her off her feet. Barely hanging on, she slammed the net to the ground then stood fearfully on the handle while the wasp thrashed at the other end like a fly in a spider's web.

The second wasp landed on Duncan's back and viciously bit into his lower left shoulder. He cried out and Alex smashed it off, then rushed to inspect the damage.

"Oh, babe. He got you good. And, oh no, that was the female. She stung you, too." She retrieved some clean strips of cloth from her pack plus a tiny jar of foul smelling liquid which she trickled into the wound, all the while keeping an eye on the skeletal predator as it chirped and spasmed on the ground.

Kara also stared as it struggled back onto its feet by furiously flapping its crippled wings. She shook her map onto the ground then pointed the bottle as the bug lurched into the air. With a weird squeaking sound, it distorted slightly, was pulled off course and *thoomp!* quickly sucked into the bottle. Kara jammed in the cork.

"And just like that, Kara's caught dinner again!" Alex announced, trying to make the best of the situation.

"Dinner?!"

"Ya like lobster?" she asked.

Kara nodded, taken aback.

"Same thing, with a little brining of course. And you know, when dragons eat them, they eat the shell and stinger, too."

"Ewww..." winced Kara, then, "I've never seen them so big."

"A breeding pair." Duncan flinched as Alex started putting bandages on. "Those holes are where they were laying their eggs."

Kara looked at him with obvious distress in her eyes, "Does it hurt?"

"Yeah, a little. They're not friendly like the bees."

Alex finished the dressings, "Okay big guy, you're done."

The trio began traveling again and, within a few steps, passed a patch of half-eaten plants.

"Ah, of course," said Alex, "that's why the wasps were here. Look at all the wild peas and carrots. They love those."

"Just like our garden at home. That's why I'm always on bug patrol. Mom and Dad say I'm an expert." Kara started singing, "The grubs eat the roots so we gotta root 'em out…" and Alex started whistling along.

When they finished their duet, Alex said, "I thought you didn't know that dragons ate bugs?"

"What?" said Kara, caught off guard.

"Well, that's the song that dragons teach their young when they're first learning to hunt."

"Oh. Wait…wow," said Kara, reviewing the song, her mind racing from surprise to reflection to understanding as all the pieces fell into place. "Wow," she concluded.

Stopping Here

A little while later, Alex noticed Duncan stumble. "Okay, we're stopping here."

Duncan laid down where he was standing and curled up on his side, shaking and sweating.

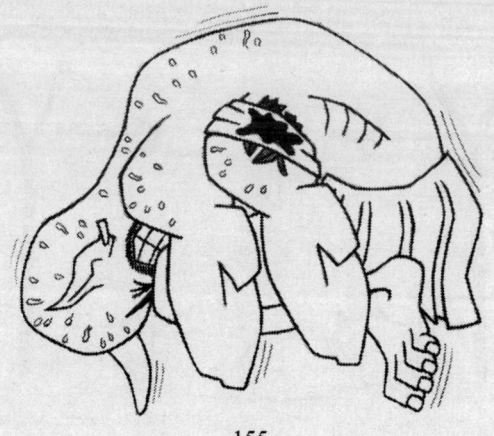

Alex pulled the tarp from his belt, shook out some residual rainwater and used it as a blanket to cover him. Kara removed her cloak and handed it to Alex who rolled it up and put it under his head, then gently stroked his brow.

"We'll need a good fire," she said, "I'll be right back."

Kara knelt by Duncan and tentatively stroked his forehead. His eye fluttered open.

"Thank you Kara. That helps a lot," he said with effort, before his eye fell shut once more.

Alex reappeared carrying an armload of branches. Kara jerked her hand back, worried she shouldn't have been doing Alex's job.

"Oh Sweetie, don't stop. He really likes that."

She leaned back in, determined to be the most perfect forehead stroker ever.

Alex built up a roaring fire then slid one of the

Stopping Here

wasps onto a long skewer and propped it up over the flames. No one spoke for a long time except for the occasional whimper from trembling unconscious Duncan.

Finally, after placing a hand on his feverish brow, Alex turned away, her expression cracking. "I'll be back. I need to get more medicine for the wound," she said over her shoulder.

Kara was really scared. "Oh Duncan, I'm so sorry you're hurt. It's all my fault," she said, barely above a whisper. "I shouldn't have been poking at those holes." She could feel her chest tightening. "I didn't expect this...to be...to be so dangerous.

"I mean, maybe we shouldn't be doing this at all," she continued, partly for him, partly for herself, and partly because the quiet was unbearable. "Maybe, if you can get so hurt, if...I mean, you're so big and I'm so small...please don't die," her voice trailed off as she choked on a sob. "Alex would be so sad if you died." Her shoulders shook as tears welled up and rolled down her cheeks.

Minutes that felt like hours had passed when Alex returned with something wrapped in a big leaf. "Kara, can you hold this please?"

"But this is honey," she protested, shocked.

"It's okay," said Alex, though she still looked very worried. Squatting down, she peeled away bloody pieces of cloth, explaining, "The bite is infected and honey is sterile. It should help him heal faster."

"Ohh..."

She pulled a burning branch from the fire, shook off the ashes then pressed its glowing tip against the wound, cringing as it sizzled. Kara jumped back, repulsed. Duncan barely moved.

Next, she carefully laid some cut herbs on the charred flesh, took the honey back and smeared it on top then tied on fresh bandages.

When she was done, she handed Kara's cloak back, knelt down with her hooves tucked under, and cradled Duncan's head in her lap.

Kara sat close, leaning on Alex's shoulder and, though the cloak had been made to fit a little girl, did her best to wrap the cape's thin material around them both, a small barrier against the evening chill. She looked up questioningly but was hesitant to say anything. Instead, she retrieved the wasp from its skewer, and they ate in silence, tossing pieces of shell into the fire.

After a while, Alex began softly whistling a low passionate tune. Her quiet melody filled the darkening forest as she stared, unfocused, at the dancing flames. When her last quavering note faded, Kara finally spoke.

"Alex, can I ask you a question?"

"Oh Kara, of course."

Stopping Here

"How'd you get these scars on your back?"

"Oh. That was from an accident. I fell…and there was fire."

Kara was quiet again, then, "Can I ask you another question?"

"Mm-hmmm?"

"When we first met, why weren't you wearing a top?"

Alex almost laughed in spite of herself, "Oh, well, sweetie… I'm a satyr. It's just kind of natural for us. Just like dragons, they don't wear clothes either."

"Huh. Okay," she said, satisfied. "But what about Duncan? He wears a skirt."

"Hahaha! Actually, it's called a kilt. And don't tell him I said this, but I think he wears it 'cuz it makes him feel pretty."

Kara snorted, "Pretty?!" then giggled, for a brief moment forgetting her fear. The silence slowly crept back in, enveloping them in its uncomfortable embrace. "Is he gonna die?"

"He's big. He'll be okay," Alex said, pensive but resolved.

They sat still for a long time, the flames licking the air above them, Duncan shivering. Eventually Kara slid down and rested her head on the edge of Alex's full lap.

Careful not to disturb her companions, Alex

fed branches from their pile to keep the fire going through most of the night. She finally dozed off toward dawn, her head and forearm resting on Duncan's clammy cheek.

Stopping Here

Only embers remained as daybreak's first light revealed a thin column of smoke rising straight into a windless sky. Duncan shifted and Alex awoke with a start, immediately placing her hand on his forehead. "Baby? How're ya feeling?"

Kara rubbed her eyes, yawned, then suddenly sat up remembering where she was and what had happened.

Duncan moaned, weakly pushed the tarp away and mumbled, "I think something died in my mouth."

Alex exhaled sharply, smiled, and choked up all at the same time. Duncan rolled to his hands and knees, then stiffly struggled to gain his feet.

"Can I help?" she asked.

"Nooo, I gotta pee." He lumbered painfully toward the bushes.

"Is he okay?" Kara asked.

"Oh yeah, he can take care of that by himself."

"What? No! I didn't mean…" Embarrassed by the misunderstanding, Kara covered her mouth and tried not to laugh. Alex caught on and laughed out loud.

"Is he better?" Kara clarified.

"It looks like the worst is over. As a matter of fact, he's probably gonna be real hungry. Ya wanna help me find some apples?"

"What about the other lobster? I mean wasp."

"I think we'll save that for later," Alex replied.

Sambuka Black

Northern Port City

Cresting the last high peak, the squat industrial city came into view. Billowing smoke stacks protruded from many of the buildings and the streets were bustling but too far away to make out any other details.

Kara wrinkled her nose, "It smells kinda bad."

"It's a bad place," sighed Duncan.

Quiet and cautious and sweating in the midday heat despite the shading canopy, they picked their way through the hilly forest for several hours before emerging on a small rise overlooking the harbor.

"Okay, time to get dressed," directed Alex as she started pulling costumes out of a well-traveled trunk.

Refilling the trunk with his kilt, belt and accoutrements, Duncan adorned his top half with a garishly colored jester's outfit including a fake arm, little dangly fake legs and a spiky bell-tipped cap. He then grabbed two pair of carved wooden hooves to disguise his feet and lower hands, and slid a beautifully crafted, papier-mâché horse head puppet over his upper left hand. He placed the reins into the fake left hand then dropped down on all fours, bending his back severely, giving the impression of a small jester with a big head on a medium sized horse.

The horse tossed its head and pawed the ground while Duncan stroked its silky mane, "Whoa there pretty girl!"

Kara couldn't believe what she was seeing and just when she thought the elaborate façade couldn't get any better, Duncan donned a purple bandit mask over his one big eye creating a comical illusion of two separate but extremely crossed eyes.

"Ha ha!" giggled Kara slyly, "but can you wink?"

Duncan contorted his face this way and that, trying to arch his eyelid to one side.

"Oh no, no babe. Your face'll get stuck that way," interjected Alex, then, "Hop on up, little lady," as she patted the bench. "It's time for me to work my magic." Kara jumped up and sat down, swinging her legs in anticipation.

Alex rifled through a small wooden box, picking out this and that, and when she looked back up, Duncan was painting something pink on Kara's face.

"Duncan, come on now. She doesn't need a caterpillar moustache. That's only funny to you." She shooed him away and wiped off the paint, then started some decorating of her own.

"First, some nice rosy cheeks I think," her skilled fingers brushing on just the right amount of blush. "Then some bright red lips to match your cape, and some light green shadow to match your eyes. And finally, we'll top it off with the ever popular, pointy princess hat. Oh yes, very pretty!" Kara beamed as Alex admired her handiwork.

Already half dressed in her harlequin costume with big poofy pants and knee high platform boots which nicely disguised her kinked furry legs, Alex covered her exposed purple skin with an exotic make up that gave her a ghostly pinkish hue.

She applied spidery fake eyelashes to her right eye, slipped on a short black wig to cover her ears and a bowler hat to hide her horns. A feather boa and elbow length gloves completed the ensemble.

Duncan looked on admiringly as Alex sashayed

toward him and threw a blanket, complete with attached horsetail, over his back.

"Alex, can I ask you a question?" asked Kara.

"Of course."

"What happened when the raccoons came running out?"

Duncan and Alex both laughed out loud.

"Oh sweetie! That's a story for when you're a bit older," she said, hopping onto Duncan's back to sit sidesaddle. "Are we ready?"

Kara swung around to sit sidesaddle on the bench, "Ready!" she confirmed.

"Giddy up Quadrapus!" cried Alex, whacking Duncan on his flank with a riding crop.

"Giddy up Mr. Woods, follow that horse!" cried Kara as they began to make their way down the hill.

"Hey, Kara?" Duncan asked.

"Un huh?"

"Yesterday, when you were poking at those holes?"

"Yeah…"

"You probably saved Alex's life, and your own as well."

"What? Really?"

"Yep. Without your warning, things could've been much, much worse. If you hadn't found those holes… I don't know what I would have done if… Thanks for helping us."

Kara was overwhelmed and speechless.

It was late afternoon by the time they reached the outer wall of the city, but from what they could hear, the street vendors inside were still in full swing. As they approached the arched stone entrance, they noticed posters on the walls.

"Uh oh," said Duncan, glancing nervously around at the luckily empty road. "That's not good. Your parents must be really worried."

Kara was conflicted. "Well, they'll just have to worry for now. Our mission is more important."

"What if someone recognizes you?" he fretted.

"Not a problem," Alex said confidently. "We can fix this. First we need to stash the red cape." She then gave Kara her boa and replaced the princess hat with a long curly auburn wig. "There. We'll make you a gorgeous redhead."

"Like my mom!"

Northern Port City

"Perfect!"

Inside the iron gates, the streets were lined with buildings, storefronts and merchants peddling their wares. Entertainers were mingling, acting funny and clanking tip jars. Richly dressed shop owners, however, seemed more interested in preening and gossiping than actually trading their goods. Dragons were everywhere.

In Kara's hometown, there were only two working dragons, a green for the main transport of supplies to and from the village, and a big beautiful blue who was rented out for large moving or building endeavors. They were both healthy and well looked after and she had watched the blue many times considering her dad was the town's only architect and was present at all its major construction projects.

Here, though, the dragons didn't look so good. Some were struggling to pull carts of heavy supplies, some were firing boilers or forges or kilns. Some were being whipped even though they were working at the steady pace their dazed eyes set them on. None of them looked happy, and most of them seemed way too skinny.

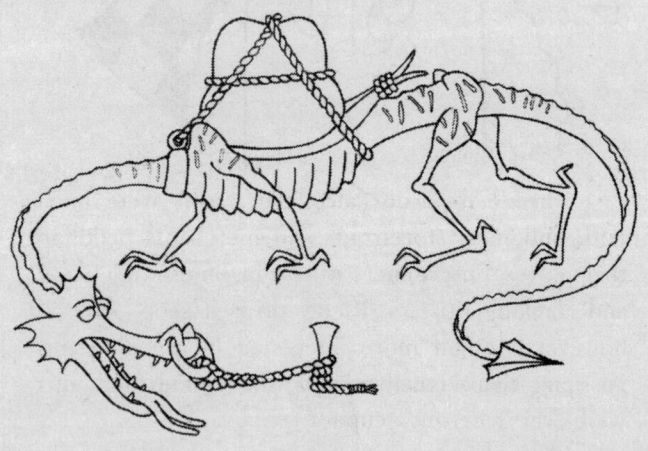

Northern Port City

As the trio strolled the market square, people turned their heads and stared with amused interest. Alex was smiling and winking at the men as she slowly spun the riding crop between her fingers. The jester entertained by performing sleight-of-hand tricks. He would fan out a deck of cards, then, with a quick flick of the wrist, miraculously replace them with three round rocks precariously pinched between his fingers. These were rolled around in his palm then tossed in the air and *poof!* they exploded into a blizzard of confetti while a deck of cards once again appeared in his hand.

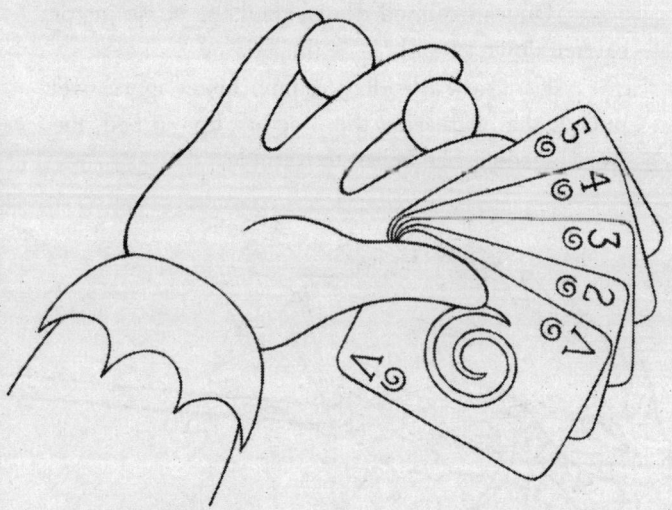

He did this several times to various passers by while Alex held out a cup for coins.

They passed a very gaunt dragon, his hips and ribs jutting, his tongue hanging out in a pant. Kara was aghast.

They passed a man hawking honey sticks and the horse started acting up and whinnying. Duncan's masked eyes darted back and forth.

Kara's eyes darted over to a tired old dragon struggling to pull a cartful of bricks.

Duncan stroked his anxious horse's jaw, "Whoa, easy there girl."

Alex stroked Duncan's jaw and fed him a sugar cube, "Whoa, easy there boy," she said.

Duncan calmed down, then the horse puppet calmed down as well.

Kara saw a bridled dragon being aggressively pulled, the bit tearing the dragon's lips so bad, they were bleeding. She began to tremble.

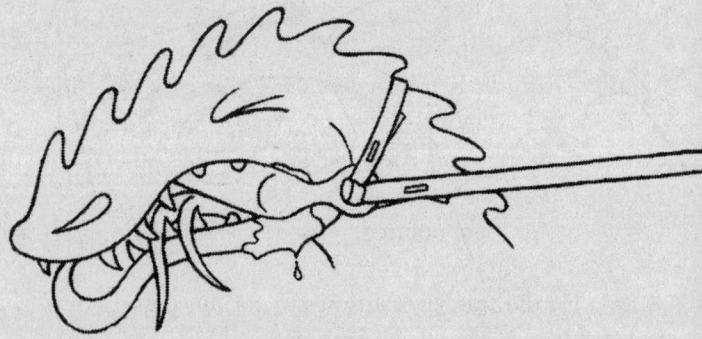

With a loud whinny, the horse gave one final toss of its head and they were past the honey stick stall.

"I'm very proud of you," Alex said quietly in her jester's ear. He smiled proudly as his horse held its head a little higher and began prancing down the street.

Kara gasped loudly as she saw a dragon being beaten bloody with a long cane.

Alex finally noticed her distress and spoke like a ventriloquist through her smile, "Kara, you have to be calm now."

The jester rolled his fingers and, seemingly out of thin air, produced a red silk rose. He presented it to a group of young ladies who smiled and curtsied while the horse bowed. Duncan whispered conspiratorially over his shoulder, "No one suspects a thing."

Kara saw a man in a blood splattered apron raise a cleaver and she whipped her head back around whispering as loudly as possible, "Where are we gonna find Dragon?!"

Duncan and Alex glanced at each other and said, "We don't know for sure..." "but we're guessing..." then pointed over Kara's head.

The Auction

Up the steep hill, past a huge doorman, down a rock corridor, up a stone stairway, through elaborately carved archways, was the Minister's office. On a T-shaped iron perch sat dazed, hypnotized Dragon.

The Minister entered his office and stepped up to one of two narrow wooden doors that flanked the far corner of the room. In a smooth, well-practiced flow, he opened the closet door, removed his coat and hat and placed them on a hangar and shelf, respectively, and closed the door. Then, gripping the edge of the heavy drapery that framed his office window, he began walking it past the sun filled glass.

In the center of the room was a stone dais displaying several crystal balls on silk pillows, some glowing with faces.

"Ladies and Gentlemen," said the Minister as he finished closing the velvet curtains. "Let the bidding begin."

The Auction

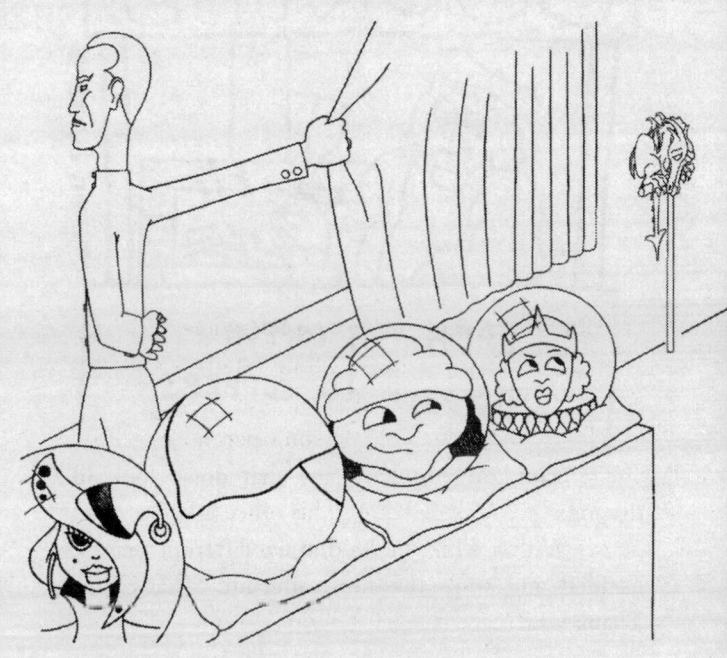

"Cookies!" cried Kara as she jumped from the bench and ran past a surprised jester, horse and harlequin then nervously approached the counter of a stall and held up a coin.

"One cookie, please."

The big friendly baker smiled and held up a dragon shaped treat. Kara chewed her lip then looked up with worried eyes.

"Um, do you have any that don't look like dragons?"

With a wink, he held out a different one. She nodded and took the new offering. "That's good. Thank you!"

The trio peeked out from behind some crates stacked just outside the cavernous loading dock. When the coast was clear, Alex took Kara by the hand and led her inside with Duncan and the bench bringing up the rear. Kara found herself being pulled along a little too insistently when *Whoosh!* a puff of flame and she saw him, Kyle, the dragon.

She balked and tried to pull away, "Alex, what's going on?"

The Auction

Alex stopped and turned. She looked down at her own hand, vexed, then released Kara.

Duncan gently put his hands on Kara's shoulders, "Let's give Alex a minute by herself okay?"

Alex steeled herself, then moved solemnly toward Kyle and held up the leftover wasp. His nostrils flared and his head slowly lowered, gently taking the wasp from her outstretched hands. She was able to briefly stroke his jaw before he went back to his mindless task.

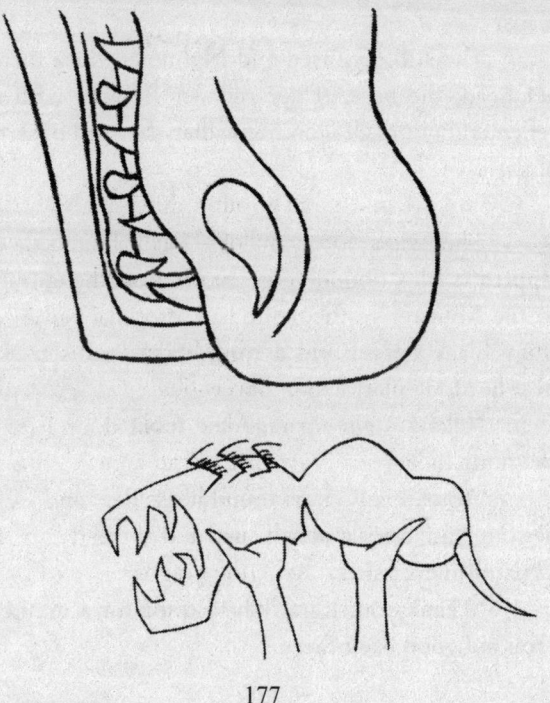

Duncan and Kara came up behind her.

"Wasps were always his favorite," she said softly.

"Are you gonna be okay?" Duncan asked.

"Yes," she said. "Yes, I'm not gonna cry," then softer, "I'm not gonna cry." Duncan stroked the top of her head as she knelt down in front of Kara, "Let's go get your Dragon."

Voices suddenly echoed from a nearby corridor. "Guards!" Duncan warned. "Change of plans."

The still confused and frightened Kara turned her head, the back of her red wig flashing with the reflected light of dragon fire as they hurried back out of the cave.

कि र औ की

The wig's loose auburn curls bounced and rippled as Alex bounded up the hill near the entrance to the Minister's office. She had also changed into a shiny black corset and a mid length crimson skirt over her long platform boots.

"Okay. Right through the front door I guess. Wish me luck."

"Your eye!" Kara reminded her and, with delicate fingers, reached up and peeled off the outlandish eyelashes.

"Thank you, Kara." She paused for a moment. "You did good back there."

The Auction

With a little difficulty, Alex straightened up as tall as possible and stepped around the corner on improbably long legs. Duncan, no longer in his costume, and Kara, now in the black wig, peeked after her. The horse head puppet, now tied to one end of the bench, appeared to stare off indifferently.

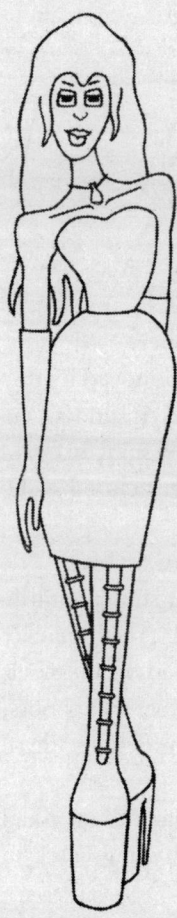

Passing under the Minister's office window, Alex approached the enormous doorman and, with the air of an elegant perfume saleswoman, poured on the flirtatiousness.

"I know the Minister has an appreciation for the finer things and I would assume his associates do as well." Her smile was infectious and, even though the guard's job was to remain professional, the corners of his mouth twitched slightly upwards. "Perhaps you'd do me the honor of sampling my most recent intoxicating aroma?"

She took out a tiny bottle and removed its tiny cork and, with her tiny hand, held it under the doorman's giant nose. He took a tiny sniff, his grin spread, his eyebrows rose and his eyes closed as he slowly slipped to the ground.

"Men are so easy," Alex chuckled.

She glanced toward the others, smiled guiltily and waved her fingers, "Hey babe!" They quickly snuck over to join her while she slipped off the skirt, gloves and wig then struggled out of her boots, complaining, "What kind of person designs these ridiculous things?"

"How are we going to get in?" Kara asked worriedly, seeing only the thinnest arching crack in

The Auction

the stone wall and a total lack of door handle.

Duncan sighed, "Okay, stand back." As he carefully shuffled toward the edge of the cliff to get a running start, Alex pushed gently on the huge, perfectly counterweighted stone door and it swung open with barely a sound.

"Much less painful," she said.

"Touché," he admitted.

The girls entered, Kara whispering, "Wow, I thought this was going to be a lot harder."

"Don't be fooled," cautioned Alex, more to herself than Kara. "We can't get comfortable. The Minister has no mercy."

Duncan, with some difficulty, dragged the bulky doorman through the entrance and into the rocky corridor, propping his lolling head against the wall. "And we've never been inside the Minister's office," he grunted, "we don't know what lies ahead." Then, to the bench, he added, "Alright Nellie, you stay here and guard the guard for us." Noiselessly, the door swung shut and a hard shadow crossed their faces, blanketing them in darkness.

"Nellie?"

Sambuka Black

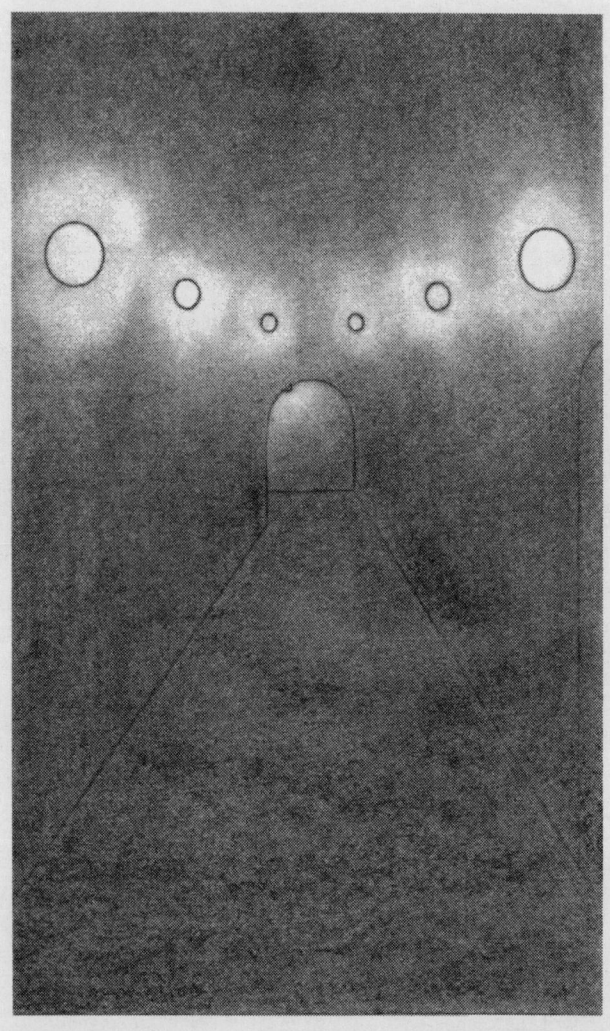

The Minister's Lair

The dimness of the Minister's office was highlighted by two crystal balls that glowed with the faces of the remaining bidders.

"I will add a hand mirror of flawless ebony from Southern San d'El, the handle inlayed with polished obsidian, and a reflective surface of incomparable perfection." The fancy dressed man raised an eyebrow at the woman in the hat pulsing in the sphere next to him.

"I must concede." She bowed her head slightly and her image faded.

"The usual arrangements, then," said the Minister and he waved the final crystal clear before the man could reply. He walked past the red rock wall to the other side of his office and documented the transaction in a fine gold embossed ledger.

Duncan and Alex crept along, carefully feeling their way as they checked for traps and alarms, moving ever deeper into the mountain. As their eyes adjusted, they saw that dim, glass covered light sources were embedded in the red rock corridor, casting them in an eerie glow.

"How do they work?" wondered Kara, studying the round ripply surfaces. "Holes drilled from outside? Mirrors reflecting torchlight? Trapped fireflies? Or maybe just a magic…"

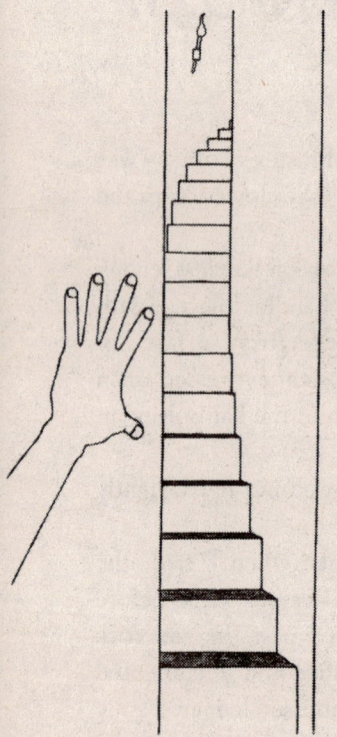

Her thoughts were interrupted when she noticed a thin crack in the wall. Pushing gently, she opened another rock door that revealed an ascending staircase.

"Hey you guys!" she called in a loud whisper, but Duncan and Alex were already far ahead and disappearing around a corner. She rushed to catch up and saw Duncan approach a heavy wooden door with a small barred opening.

The Minister's Lair

He glanced in, then jumped back as if burned, looking fearful and disgusted. Alex, stretching tall to look, reacted the same way. Duncan continued down the hallway, giving a wide berth to another similar door.

"What's in there?" Kara asked.

"Not your dragon," Alex answered, "We can't help him."

"Him?"

"Just-- He's-- Come on, we have to keep moving." She hurried past, but Kara's curiosity got the better of her.

She gripped the bottom sill of the little window and pulled herself up onto her tiptoes, just barely able to peek in. With lightning speed, a pale withered hand reached out and grabbed the back of her head, crushing her face against the door. Then came a squishy gurgling moan and a dead looking tentacle whipped out, snaked around her left arm and violently yanked it back through the bars, lifting her clear off the floor.

Her throat opened wide, sucking in air to scream.

A hand slapped over her mouth and another shot past her head and gripped her attacker. Alex's axe like hooves bit into the rough splintery door, her fingers digging into the coiling sinewy flesh of the hideous prisoner.

"Duncan! Duncan, help!" she desperately whispered. He rushed back and, grappling with all four hands, finally pulled them free. They collapsed heavily against the opposite wall in a tangled heap.

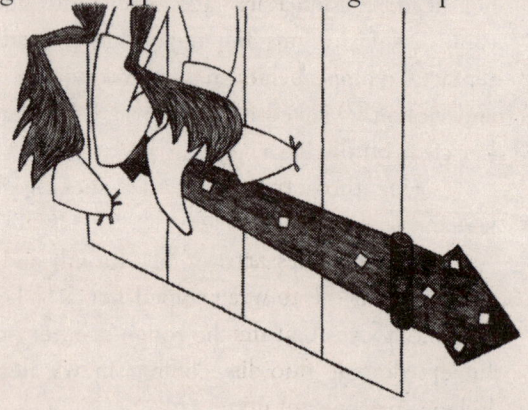

The Minister's Lair

Alex was still wrapped around Kara, "Can you be quiet? You have to be quiet!" Bloody, tears streaming, Kara nodded her head but a small strangled sound still escaped as Alex dropped her hand away.

They inspected Kara's split forehead while Alex ripped a piece of cloth for a bandage. "We have to stop the bleeding."

"No, no, not that!" Kara wheezed between fractured sobs, "My shoulder! My shoulder!"

"Oh Kara," Duncan empathized, "Okay. This is gonna hurt." With Alex again covering Kara's mouth, he quickly, but as gently as possible, forced her shoulder back into place. A muffled scream disappeared down the dark passageway, shadowed by his darting eye.

He hugged Kara close, cooing, "It's okay. It's over now. The first time's always the worst." She gritted her teeth behind pursed lips trying to breathe slowly and evenly through her nose while he rocked her gently back and forth.

Using the strip of cloth, Alex skillfully folded and twisted and tied, making a comfortable sling that immobilized Kara's arm across her chest, then tore off another piece to wrap her forehead.

"What is that thing?" Kara shuddered.

Alex was too disturbed to answer and instead asked, "Can you get up now? We have to go."

Kara winced, "Yeah. Yeah."

"We can't go any farther that way," said Duncan. "It's all bricked up now."

"There's another door," Kara offered, "back there. We passed it when we came in."

The trio retraced their steps then followed the narrow stone stairs upward to a second level.

Duncan stealthily stepped out into the hall and saw two elaborately carved archways that led into a large room. He also saw the mounted heads of many creatures lining the outer corridor. He jumped back, horrified, and flattened himself against the wall, his staring eye unfocused. All the stories were true! He tried to swallow but his throat was suddenly dry. "Oh, no…"

Alex leaned past him and saw the trophy heads, "Holy cursss…" she trailed off under her breath, sick to her stomach.

"What is it?!" Kara asked, though not so anxious to look this time.

"We have to get out of here!" hissed Duncan, hysteria writhing like snakes in his belly.

"Shhh, shhh, be calm," Alex soothed, gently placing a hand on his chest. "We can do this. Is anyone in there?"

Duncan closed his eye and was still for a moment before slowly, very slowly, peering around the edge of the doorway.

The Minister's Lair

Completely unaware of the inconceivable surveillance, the Minister finished his notes then paused in front of one of his most prized possessions, a thick wooden plaque that displayed a magnificent pair of muscular outstretched arms. Even after decades of countless viewings, this early acquisition still filled him with pride and nostalgia.

Duncan saw none of this in the thin slice of office his awkward vantage point allowed. Then, a fleeting glimpse of movement and he jerked his head back, trying to pretend his heart wasn't racing as the Minister exited the far archway and strode off down the hall.

When the sharp click of footsteps faded away, Duncan scurried out, waving the others to follow, and together with Alex, tried to shield Kara from the horrific head collection. Kara in turn tried not to look, but did anyway, and immediately wished she hadn't.

Sambuka Black

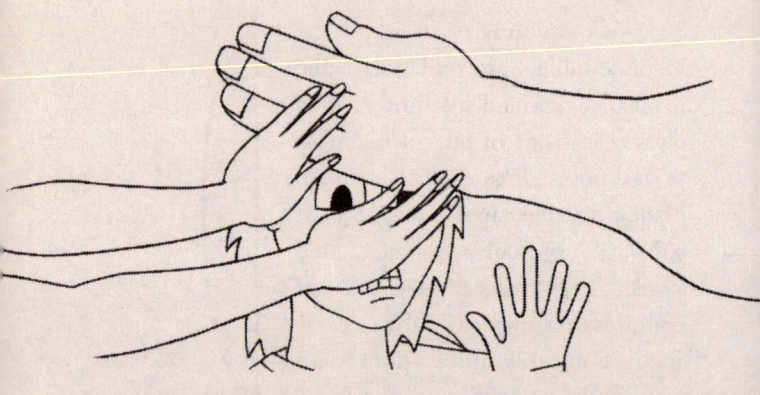

They stole into the office where Duncan and Alex split up to guard the archways. Kara ran over to Dragon and struggled with her one good arm to pull him from the perch but his feet were locked in a death grip.

"He won't let go!" she whispered urgently.

Duncan stepped toward her, "We'll tear out the whole perch then."

"Too noisy! Too noisy!" croaked Alex, frantically waving him back to his post. "Kara! Just do the spell now!"

Moving as quickly and quietly as she could, Kara pulled out her little bowl, took off the lid, pulled out the bottle of vaporizing agent, used her teeth to pull out the cork, spat it on the ground, then poured a drop of the liquid into the crushed up mixture.

The Minister's Lair

There was a low crackling and she flinched away as a puff of smoke erupted in her face leaving it covered in a layer of fine white ash. She blinked her eyes and shook her head and exhaled sharply trying to blow the caustic smell out of her nostrils.

She looked at Dragon; he looked the same.

She looked in her bowl; there were bits of charcoal and a partly melted gold button.

She looked at Alex. "It didn't work," came her small voice.

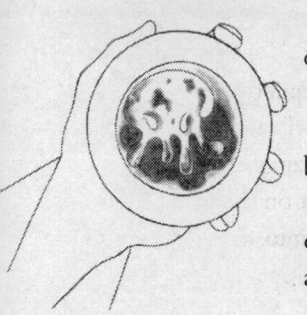

"What?" Duncan asked over his shoulder.

"Do it again!" Alex urged.

"I can't!" said Kara breathlessly, "It's all burned up."

Without warning, the door next to the closet opened and the Minister gently shouldered his way into the room, his ledger tucked neatly under one arm, a bowl of yogurt and granola in one hand and a long, delicate silver spoon in the other.

Everyone froze.

A crunchy dollop halfway to his mouth, the Minister's eyes darted from satyr to cyclops to dragon to girl. "YOU!" he shouted, dropping his book and bowl and spattering his beautiful clothes with yogurty goo.

Kara squealed and ran to hide behind the dais as Duncan and Alex lunged. The Minister threw out his hands and the pair lifted from the ground kicking and screaming.

Duncan drifted in front of the trophy arms creating a momentary illusion of his younger self, while Alex fanned at the cloud of smoke bomb she'd thrown too late.

The Minister's nose twitched with the memory of Alex's hoof just as one of her thrashing legs inadvertently knocked two of his crystal balls from their pillowed pedestal to shatter on the stone floor.

The Minister's Lair

"Not...again!" he roared. Scowling and straining, he maneuvered the attackers away from his precious collection, but seemed weakened by the years as they lurched inexorably closer. His fingers flexed and grasped but he was losing control when an odd sensation tickled through him. He was light, like a feather floating on a breeze while the satyr and cyclops became taller and taller but were moving away somehow. His body felt stretchy and twisted and the girl had grown to gargantuan proportion as she loomed up behind him when...

Thoomp! It worked!

She was so shocked, she almost slipped in the spilled eyeballs as she jammed the cork back in, barely noticing the pain in her shoulder, then held the bottle out at arm's length as if it might explode.

"Kara! You did it!" yelled Alex as she ran over and immediately began retying the loosened sling.

Duncan, speechless, squatted down to stare at the miniature Minister who leapt and waved and shrieked and cursed while streaks of viscous yellow fluid trickled down the inside of the glass tube. Ignoring the squeaking tirade and nodding as his giant grin spread, he looked up at Kara's pallid face and finally said, "Simple as sou-"

Joyous peeping and a flurry of wings interrupted the wise insight as Dragon fluttered onto Kara's shoulder. She shoved the bottle at Duncan, who grabbed it with three hands just for good measure, then wrapped her arm around Dragon and snuggled him up as he cried, *Cookie! Cookie! Cookie!*

She reached into her pocket and pulled out the Minister shaped delicacy, "I thought you might be hungry!"

Dragon fanned out his wings and chirped before he tore off the head and munched voraciously.

Facing each other, Duncan and Alex both snapped to attention. Over Alex's shoulder on the far wall were two of the most beautiful things Duncan

The Minister's Lair

had ever seen.

"Kyle!" exclaimed Alex, jumping up.

"Huh?" His thoughts jerked sideways, "You don't think?!..."

They rushed from the room, Duncan vaulting the dais to the detriment of yet another crystal ball.

"Hey! Where are you...wait for us!" Kara cried after them, cradling Dragon as she struggled to her feet and clumsily gathered her belongings.

Outside again, Duncan and Alex surveyed the blocky silhouette of the city. Distant yelling and crashing and giant puffs of dust suggested a great deal of commotion and confusion. A couple of dragons' heads bobbed above rooftops and, circling above them, a dragon couple bobbed and weaved recalling their first flirtatious flight.

They smiled so hard, their cheeks began to ache and by the time Kara joined them on the wide ledge, Alex was ecstatic and unable to contain herself. "You did it Kara! You really did it! They're free! ALL OF THEM!"

Secluded in Dragon's world of trilling and ear licking, Kara still wasn't comprehending the scope of her accomplishment.

Alex wrapped her arms around the two as Duncan boomed, "Come on, we have to get Kyle!" in the happiest voice she'd heard in years.

Completely forgetting the loyal bench, he scooped her up as she held Kara who held Dragon and sprinted back down the pathway toward the cavern below, kilt, wings and hearts aflutter.

Just as they were about to reenter the loading dock, a gigantic, ground shaking green shape landed heavily behind them.

Hey you two! Who's your friend?

They spun around and Kyle added, *or should I say, friends?*

The Minister's Lair

"Kyle!" squealed Alex as she sprang forward and leapt onto his thick neck then shuddered as years worth of guilt poured out.

Kyle delicately wrapped his huge talons around her, *It's good to see you, too Miss Alex,* came his deep rich voice, resonating through them all.

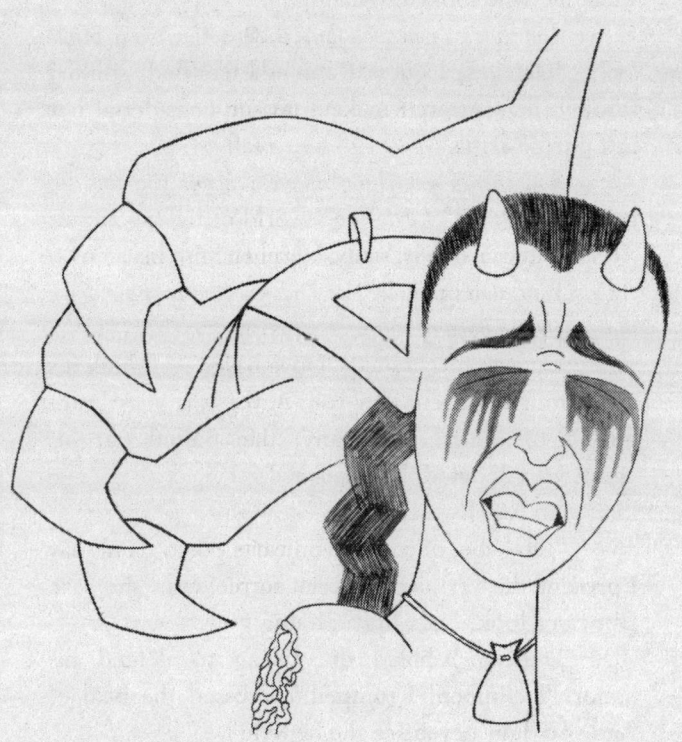

Duncan too ran up and embraced his friend. "It's been forever!"

That long? Yes... Something unusual has happened, observed Kyle. He gently lowered Alex back to the ground while she continued to cling and weep. Kara was amazed that so many tears could come out of someone who looked so happy.

And that's a new look for you, Miss Alex. You're pink!

"Uh, yes, I guess I am," she sniffled, smiling through her smeared makeup as she considered her half purple arms.

And there's something different about you too, he trailed off.

Duncan slowly, sadly, began to raise his arms.

Wait, don't tell me. No! Did you finally shave down that annoying horn of yours?

Duncan brightened, "Do you like it? I think it's much more efficient this way. And I was very brave during the entire procedure." He puffed out his chest. Alex snorted. Kyle laughed.

"What? I was!"

"Oh babe, of course you were," then, "and may I present the very smart, very heroic and," she gave Duncan a look, "very brave, Kara."

Duncan babbled on, trying to defend his honor, "I climbed! I jumped! I crossed the bridge! And you didn't even see the big eye!"

Kyle continued to chuckle, low and rumbly,

The Minister's Lair

Yes, I can see you're looking a bit frayed, then turning and bowing his head, *An honor to meet you, Kara.*

"Who we need to return to her worried parents," Alex added, "Care to join us?"

I'd offer you all a ride, but I seem to be a bit frayed myself. He flapped his deformed wing. *And what of Silas? Did you find him?*

Duncan and Alex looked at each other, hesitating. "He…We…" they stammered together.

Slowly and quietly, Alex said, "He passed away many years ago." Then, after carefully untying the pouch at her neck, she held up Silas' eye patch. Kyle gently touched it with his snout, closing his eyes for a moment.

I will remember him. Miss Alex, will you take care of that for me until we return home? He turned back, *Now, who's little purple here?* Dragon scampered down from Kara's shoulder and over to Kyle, stretching up tall on his hind legs until they were almost nose to nose. *All I'm getting is 'cookie, cookie, cookie.'*

"Actually, he doesn't have a real name yet. I was thinking-" Kara was interrupted by a sudden gasp as Duncan bounded away.

The northern lights played across a violet vista to the fading sounds of chaos in the city. Lighthearted footsteps approached a rise in the dirt road as five friends began their journey home, together and free.

Sambuka Black

In the lead was Dragon who scampered, paused, flapped, sniffed, hopped, paused again, flew around in a circle, then repeated the whole process. Next were Kyle and Duncan on either side with the girls strolling in between, followed by the bench, its horse head held high and facing backwards.

"Or what about something cute? Like Puff, or Norbert?" Alex was saying.

Or perhaps something intellectual, like Draco? suggested Kyle.

"I was thinking something elegant, like Prince, or Q," said Kara.

"You mean like the letter?" asked Alex.

Duncan turned to the others, maneuvering his mounted trophy arms so they wouldn't knock into anyone, "No, no! He needs something tough and intimidating like," in a growly voice, "Vermithrax! Or Pauuuuuul!"

What is it with you and the name Paul? Kyle inquired, *Let me guess, the bench's name is Paul.*

Duncan, wide-eyed, turned towards Kyle in a moment of epiphany and opened his mouth to speak.

"I know, what about Cookie?" said Alex.

"But isn't Cookie kind of a girl's name?" Kara wondered.

Wait a minute, said Kyle, *How old is little purple anyway?…*

Dragon paused, sitting up, before disappearing

The Minister's Lair

over the crest of the hill and down to join the others, followed only by the tip of Kyle's sweeping tail.

Aftermath

The light blue dragon found himself in the city with only a vague recollection of what he had been doing; he did not recognize his surroundings. Gazing about, he smiled when he saw a familiar face, then stepped over to the delicately featured green female. They rubbed noses and looked deep into each other's eyes.

The horse sized dragon galloped joyfully, pulling a bouncing produce cart and leaving a trail of cabbages and carrots and gourds and beets. A man was giving chase, yelling and pleading and grabbing his hair in despair. He picked up a damaged pumpkin and threw it back down at the ground in frustration as his cart passed him again, speeding in large circles.

Aftermath

The tall starving dragon ate greedily from the cart's spilling goods. A man continued to whack her flank with a stick, but this time, she simply swished her tail like a horse swatting at flies. The man sailed across the square and crashed into some baskets of grain, arms and legs akimbo.

Slipping, almost falling, on the smooth stone floor, Duncan rushed around the corner and through the archway. He couldn't believe he'd almost forgotten. Reaching out, he reverently lifted the glass dome and released the little Bobbykin who stepped carefully onto his strong hand and gripped a finger for balance. He scanned the floor for its eyes and saw that one was squashed flat under a sticky footprint. The other, though, was undamaged and reseated perfectly into its socket. Duncan promised the little skeleton he'd stop the poisoning and help it reunite with its clan. He also assured that one could get by very nicely with only one eye.

With its sharp incisors, the big red carnivale dragon snipped the bonds of the little red veal dragons who jubilantly jumped about. When Gran saw the young ones gather like chicks around a mother hen, her heart swelled and she raided her small greenhouse for all its tender sweet flowers.

The little red veal dragons were playing the most wonderful game. They'd lifted the Wheel of Doom from its stand and were rolling it back and forth while the butcher and barker yelled and scrambled clumsily to stay on top. The reds barked and chirped with delight as the wheel careened off the road, down the hill and into the stream. The soaking wet men ran off down the road and the bouncy reds joined in the game of catch.

Aftermath

The giant blue was in the middle of a complicated lift when she happened to notice the sunset was much prettier than usual. The aqueduct system was an interesting project and as she looked toward the source of the mountain stream, she tried to recall when it had all started. It seemed like only a few days ago, but had they really accomplished so much so fast? She shrugged and went back to work. She liked moving things and in a few minutes, they'd be done for the day and her human friends would give her soothing massages and a warm oil bath.

When they approached the crevasse and Duncan started to make a fuss, Kyle looked quizzically at him then the suspension bridge. Being good friends with the Logues and familiar with their legendary construction skills, not to mention their solvent expertise, he stomped happily across while the short little bridge flapped and flopped. Without breaking. Not even a splinter. Hooting and clapping, Alex and Kara skipped after him followed by Dragon and the bench, then finally Duncan who strolled casually, pretending to not be afraid.

Her black hair and beaded costume shimmering in the moonlight, the laughing high wire gymnast squeezed her strong legs around the mother red's neck and clung to the curving backspine as they

Sambuka Black

swooped and dipped, rolled and dove. The colored lights and torches of the carnivale twinkled far below while the people cried out and pointed.

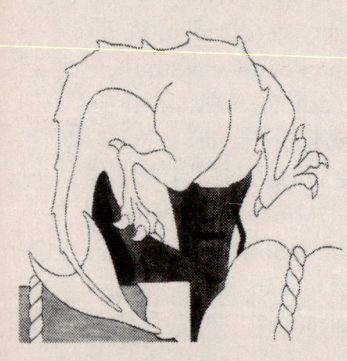

Figuring out the latch to Alex's costume trunk, Dragon was the picture of sophisticated elegance in the short black wig, but felt more confident as a gorgeous redhead and, by kicking and squirming, fit almost completely inside one of the tall black boots.

Finally back home, Kara jumped into the arms of her crying parents who instinctively jumped back and held her in a death grip when they saw the creatures who followed. She had to struggle free

Aftermath

then drag them forward to meet her new friends. Dragon immediately leapt into Mom's arms, wrapping around her neck. She instinctively hugged back, eyes wide and worried, but then completely melted when she felt a kittenish purr.

Dad found the top piece of paper on his desk to have several doodles on it. Hmm. It had been years since Kara had drawn stick pictures like that. One was of a cornhusk doll, one was of some flowers and one sort of resembled a man with his head and shoulders bitten off.

Dragon sat on the bed while Kara practiced her new instrument. She slowly swirled the metal wand around the two antennae, carefully reading the sheet music that laid between them. After a few waves of her hand and a few tremulous notes, Dragon, head thrown back, began to trill an exact imitation, finishing the melody where Kara left off.

M. and Mme. Gaudet woke up one morning to find Dragon taking a shower under the spill from their waterwheel. A surprised glance over the shoulder, and a meticulously washed armpit was an image they would recount at family gatherings for years to come.

Sambuka Black

Epilogue

Dragons flitted playfully near the plateau chortling to one another as they dove, wings tucked back, plummeting mere inches from the cliff face before pulling up just short of certain death to brush the ticklish tree tops with their bellies. Birds sang, crickets chirped, waterfalls roared, the usual cacophony of the busy forest surrounded the butte.

Beyond the thick rock wall, however, the silence was oppressive and black. A white crab scuttled past unseen. A luminescent jellyfish drifted along followed by several iridescent eels. The enormous eye retreated inside the sunken granite tube.

All was slow and calm and cold. Then, a small orange flash. Then another. Again and again, he hurled fireballs toward the distant cork. Repeatedly it flared then faded to glowing embers, briefly highlighting the rusting links of chain that wound round his glass cell and disappeared into the depths. Ragged and filthy, the Minister slogged, knee-deep, in a pool of clotting yellow ooze, screaming unheard.

Clink! and the embers went dark.

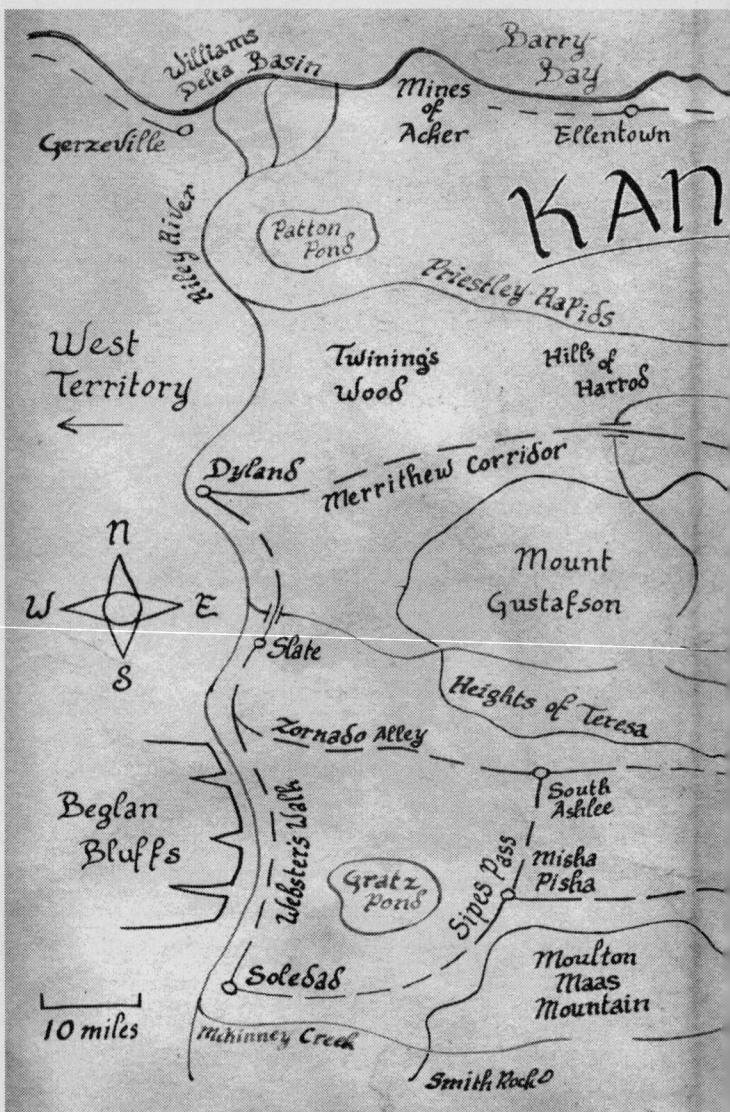

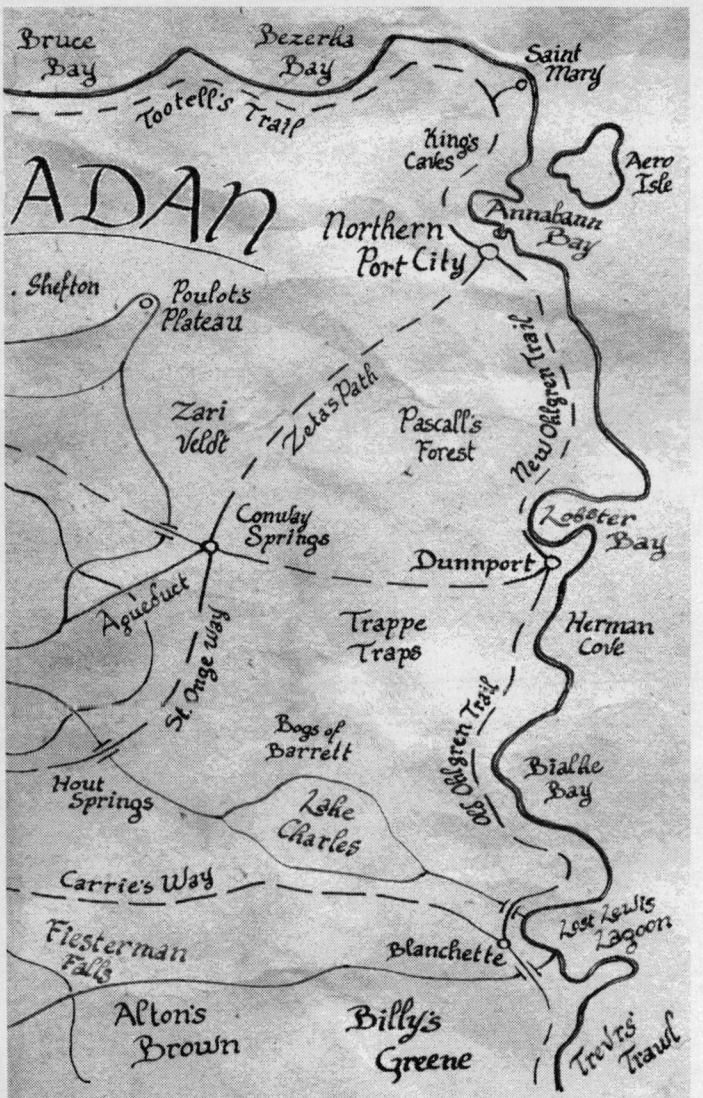

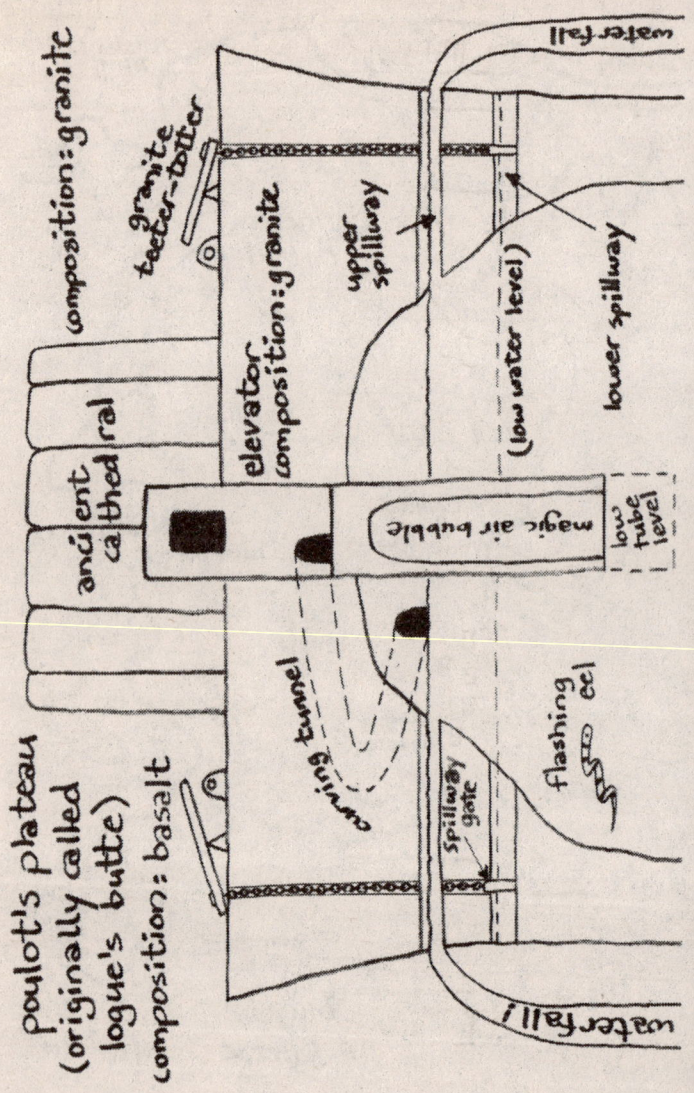

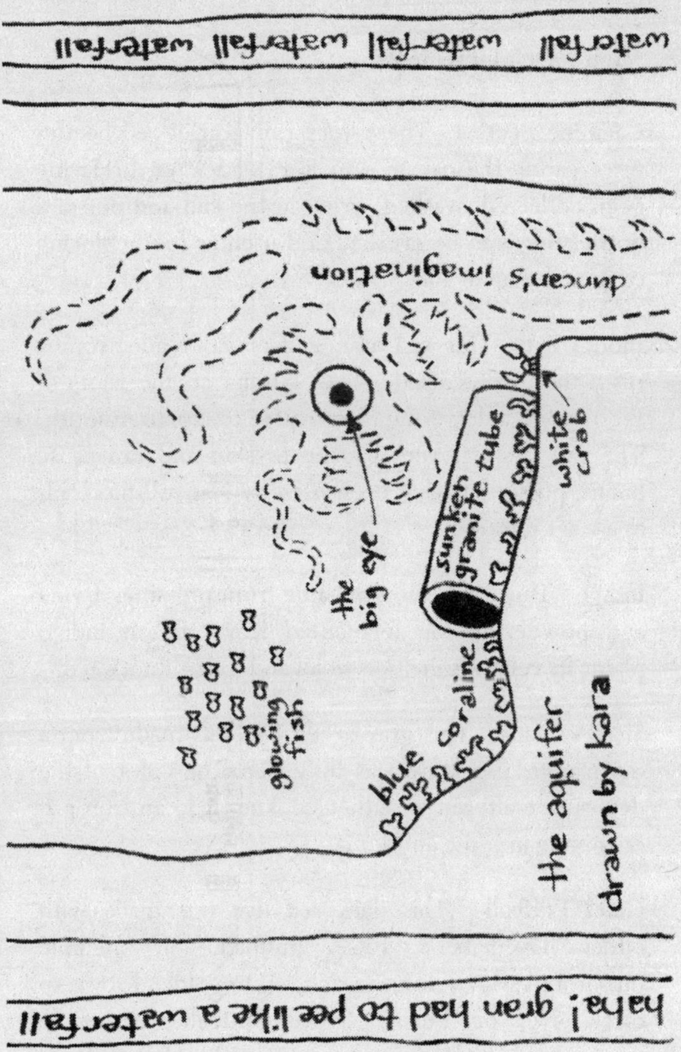
waterfall waterfall waterfall waterfall
duncan's imagination
the big eye
sunken granite tube
white crab
blue coraline
glowing fish
the aquifer
drawn by kara
haha! gran had to pee like a waterfall

Mom's Shelf Ingredients:

Carmine Beetles - These very tiny scarlet-red beetles were eating the oak tree in Kara's back yard. Having been collected, washed, dried in the sun and put in a bottle, they can be crushed and used as food coloring or in make-up or ink.

Bloodwort - This red-orange dye was made from a resin that grows inside small bumps on the roots of Bloodwort, a flowering plant native to North America. The raw resin is very caustic to skin and can cause burns, possibly having been used by Native Americans as a wart remover.

Indigo - This dark blue dye came from pressing, drying and powdering the fermented leaves of an indigo plant. Its relatives include woad and dyer's knotweed.

Shaggy Mane - This gray-green dye was made from a mushroom also known as Inky Cap. The color of the dye can be altered by either cooking it in an iron pot or mixing in some ammonia.

Giant Puffball - This dark red dye was made with either Dyemaker's False Puffball, an inedible mushroom which makes a rich red to golden brown to black dye, or Purple Spore Puffball, an edible mushroom which makes a rust red dye. It was huge and partly rotten when Kara's mom found it, so even she doesn't know which mushroom it was, but the dye is pretty.

Scaly Hedgehog - This blue-green fabric dye was made from an icky tasting mushroom also called shingled hedgehog.

Purple Snails - This purple dye was made from a specific type of sea snail. In many ancient cultures, purple was reserved for royalty because the snails were difficult to find and expensive to make into dye.

Sulfur - Historically called brimstone, this element with the symbol S was mined as yellow crystals and ground into an icky smelling powder. It can be mixed with KNO_3 and charcoal to make black powder, or with water or oil to make a yellow dye (...and, oops, Mom misspelled this label.)

Burnt Lime (aka Quicklime) - This white powder was made by heating limestone in a kiln to 850 degrees Celsius. When mixed with water, this powder can become hot enough to cause wood to burst into flame.

Slaked Lime - This white powder was made by slowly and carefully mixing Burnt Lime with water. When done properly, this can be used as a leavening agent similar to baking soda or as a preservative in pickling.

Kayen Eau Trois - This white powder was scraped from a cave wall and mixed with a liquid Mom concocted. The powder is Potassium Nitrate, a chemical compound with the symbol KNO_3. It has been known by many names throughout history such as Potash, made from storing wood ashes in a copper pot, or saltpeter, meaning "stone salt" coming from the crystalline form harvested off cave walls.

Enaych Trois - This liquid was made by cooking rotting plants with burnt lime and is Ammonia, a chemical compound with the symbol NH_3. It will darken wood by chemically reacting to the tannins inside the wood itself and can also be made by fermenting urine.

Pine Sap - Used as a wood polish, this resin was harvested by making a small cut in certain types of pine trees and collecting the sap.

Distilled Pine - Commonly known as turpentine, this solvent was made by distilling a pot of Pine Sap.

Tallow - This was made by skimming the fat off the top of a boiling pot of animal parts. The fat can be burned in lamps, used in making soap or as a leather conditioner.

Kara's firestone contains Magnesium (Mg) which is an element found in over 60 minerals. Once extracted, it will burn very hot and even under water.

Duncan's firepiston is a device found in many ancient cultures and works on the principle that when air is quickly compressed, its temperature can rise to 500F or more, plenty hot enough to ignite a small ball of fluff.

Dad's math puzzle explanation:

$$1+2+3+\ldots+49+\boxed{50}+51+\ldots+97+98+99+\boxed{100}$$

$$\left.\begin{array}{l} 1 + 99 = 100 \\ 2 + 98 = 100 \\ 3 + 97 = 100 \\ \downarrow \\ 49 + 51 = 100 \end{array}\right\} \text{that makes 49 100's}$$

$$\begin{array}{r} 4900 \\ \text{plus 100 at the end} \quad 100 \\ \text{plus 50 left over in the middle} \quad \underline{50} \\ \hline 5050 \end{array}$$

Duncan and Alex's Books:

Legends of Mythical Creatures – This is the original version of Kara's book, *Mythical Creatures - Fantasy and Fairytales*. Minister James had it re-written along with *A Dragyn's Tale* in order to push non-human creatures to the outskirts of society and justify his enslavement of dragonkind.

The Dragons Book of Myths & Secrets – This is an ode to *The Woman's Encyclopedia of Myths & Secrets* by Barbara G. Walker (©1983), a magnificent treasure of fascinating historical references explained back to their roots.

Under My Spell, A Manifesto – Written by Minister James and about as fascinating as *Mein Kempf*.

Downfall: Coppers and Golds – This is an historical account of how a previous Kanadan culture destroyed itself by elevating the need for power and wealth over that of the health of the land and its people.

David and the Keys of Catastrophe – *Catastrophe* is a book by David Keys (©1999) chronicling the worldwide catastrophes that began in 535ce (common era) with dramatic climate change, famine and plague which affected cultures from the Roman Empire to China to the Middle East to the Americas.

Claws & Lamentations —Often outrageous satirical stories written by the greatest dragon playwright, Tim of the West Peaks. His characters portray human personality traits and endlessly stumble through absurd scenarios to the delight of dragon audiences world wide.

Cyclops Whisperer — Alex's favorite book.

Le Bois — The philosophical dilemma: to use defenseless trees for one's own benefit or to allow them their own personal journey, free from the tyranny of axe and saw. This is an ode to the song, "The Trees" by RUSH. Recommended viewing: The Woodwright's Shop on PBS.

Bonne Bouffé — This is an ode to "Good Eats" with Alton Brown, a tv show mix of Julia Child, Monty Python and The Wizard.

Cooking With Grubs — Duncan's favorite book.

Fungi — Separate from plants, animals, minerals or bacteria, the Fungi Family includes molds, yeasts and mushrooms. *Mycelium Running* by Paul Stamets (©2005) explains how mushrooms can save the world.

Needles — A history of the evolution and uses of needles. From wood and pine needles to bone and quills to metal, needles have played a significant role in the development of clothing, tools and weapons, housing, tattooing, medicine and other applications too numerous to count.

Rocks & Gems — If you are interested in rocks, gems or fun science projects of every sort, we suggest checking out www.teachersource.com

Faeries — Creative methods of humanely controlling the constant hijinx of this common pest. Faeries breed like mosquitoes and during peak years (coinciding with solar maximum) the pranks, giggling and whizzing about can drive one mad. Learn to build intriguing decoys, mazes, puzzles and traps to keep the little buggers preoccupied and out of your hair.

Embrassade — Cats and Eskimos do it with their noses. Snails and wasps use their antennae. Parrots rub their beaks together. Everything kisses (especially faeries) and this encyclopedic volume covers them all.

A Fire Inside — AFI, one of Jeff's favorite bands.

Karma Shastra — If you do good things, good things

will come back to you. Apocryphal fables from those who lived them.

Where the Cobblestones End: A Collection of Dragon Poetry — If you have never read *Where the Sidewalk Ends: Poems and Drawings* by Chel Silverstein (©1974), then go out and find it right now. It is the epitome of breakthrough books for the budding poet in every child of any age.

Insects:Exotic & Mundane — The title says it all, plus lots of scary, close-up drawings.

Keeping Dirt Alive — Every spoonful of healthy soil has hundreds of thousands of micro-organisms and if they die, we die. *Teaming with Microbes* by Jeff Lowenfels & Wayne Lewis (©2010) is a must-read for anyone into nature or gardening or biology.

Soothing the Mandrake — This is an ode to Professor Sprout and her creator, J.K. Rowling.

Adam&Elliot — This is an ode to the absolutely brilliant clay animated movie "Mary & Max," by Adam Elliot (©2009). Roughly based on a true story, it chronicles the letters between two very unlikely pen-pals, an odd yet curious 5 year old in Australia and a man living with Asperger's Syndrome in New York. Dramatically charming, Adam's movie will make you cry, and smile.

L'Enfer de Dante – The Italian classic translated into French.

MMI – A reference to the book by Arthur C. Clark and the genre of prognostic science fiction. His peers include Robert A. Heinlein and Isaac Asimov.

MCMLXXXIV – A reference to the book by George Orwell that every person on earth should read. Considered by some to be as dangerous to society as books like *A Brave New World* by Aldous Huxley and *We* by Yevgeny Zamyatin, it followed his novella, *Animal Farm*, and led the way for works such as *Fahrenheit 451* by Ray Bradbury and *The Handmaid's Tale* by Margaret Atwood.

A Dragyn's Tale – This copy is signed by Kyle.

tell no tales – An album by TNT which includes "Northern Lights", a song that matches this story to a T.

Malicieux – French for *Wicked*, one of the best Broadway musicals ever.

WWJWD – What would Joss Whedon do? A question we asked ourselves many times while writing this book.

A Dragyn's Tale by Kyle the Dragon

A long time ago, In a land down below,
Made from dust and sand,
A prince and his father, Rich with water,
Searched throughout their land.

A dragon egg they sought, Many fakes they bought,
'Til at last they found their treasure.
Shimmering green, With a pearlescent sheen,
The prince was bursting with pleasure.

The day it hatched, They were matched,
Their eternal friendship was fastened.
They played and played and played for years,
Until the day it happened.

Hide and seek was the game, And no one was to blame,
But fire is unforgivable.
To startle was the aim, No one knew he could flame,
The boy's face was unrecognizable.

Though forgiven by the prince, The town was incensed,
So the sultan told the dragon he must flee.
Grief like he never knew, The adolescent beast flew,
Aimless, across the sea.

Now a mighty dragon,
He lived on a mountain top,
He would wail and wail and wail all night,
And simply would not stop.

One day came a knight, All shiny and bright,
Upon his silver steed.
All dressed in white, His sword held tight,
To do the Noble Deed.

But with one blow, Of his mighty lungs,
The dragon wiped him out.
Down and down and down he fell,
Landing with a shout,

"I'll get you dragon, I'll get you yet!
You've not seen the last of me!"
Again and again and again he tried,
'Til he was blown right out to sea.

But then came a wizard, To kill that lizard,
His magical wand in hand.
The village agreed, That he would succeed,
For he was the best in the land.

He conjured all night, Till he could ignite,
A roaring fireball.
Higher and higher and higher it climbed,
Till it reached ten feet tall.

But the wizard, Annoyed the dragon,
So he raised a mighty din,
And he dug and he dug and he dug a huge hole,
And dropped the wizard in.

Then came a boy, With a little dragon toy,
That gave the town a thought,
"We'll build a doll, Some twenty feet tall!"
That was it! The answer they'd sought!

An offering they made, Of rags and hay,
And hauled it to the dragon's cave,
They hoped and hoped and hoped it would,
Their tiny village save.

Well, the dragon was simply delighted,
For now he had a friend.
He loved and loved and loved that doll,
His lonely heart, it did mend.

Things to Ponder:

What did they finally decide to name Dragon?

Why is Dragon so rare and valuable?

What is Kara's major magic talent?

What does the title mean?

What is the name of Dad's "magically challenged" friend?

If you have read all the way to this point, we figure you probably like our book. Please let us know on facebook and tell all your friends! You can buy books directly, as well as related items, on our website, www.sambukablack.com .The more books we sell, the faster we'll be able to release the sequel.

Every book has a journey, please write on this page about its travels with you…and then pass it on to the next person so more can be written here…